I0682559

HEART OF ALBION

Triad of Albion Book Two

Stuart France & Sue Vincent

Unwittingly drawn into the mysterious and magical landscape of *The Initiate*, Don and Wen pondered the visual language of symbols, stumbling across revelations and realisations that would alter their perception of the age-old stories they thought they knew.

A hilltop steeped in tragedy, a child whose eyes see too much... a Word-Weaver's birth into darkness... strange forms shimmering on the edge of vision. They learned to walk the Living Land, listening to the whispers of Earth memory and the ghosts of the most ancient past. And from those tales, another line of communication opens as they explore the folklore, legends and traditional tales handed down, from heart to heart, over the millennia.

As the two friends travel between the sacred sites of Albion, they discover stories that tell how the leys were made, the true origins of the hillforts and the reason why Father Fish had breakfast in Slug Town.

Striding across this landscape of myth are the giants. From Cerne Abbas to the top of the Beanstalk, from Camelot to the Castle of Maidens, how and why is their presence stamped on the Living Lore of the land by their seven league boots?

Join Don and Wen as the adventure continues, unravelling its mysteries and the magical relationship between Albion and its people.

First published December 2013 as
'The Heart of Albion: Tales from the Wondrous Head'
by Stuart France & Sue Vincent

Silent Eye Press
Copyright © 2021 Sue Vincent & Stuart France
All rights reserved.
ISBN: 978-1-910478-35-6

Triad of Albion Book Two

HEART OF ALBION

STUART FRANCE & SUE VINCENT

*"The Lore of the Land, although perfect,
does not impose itself, it simply waits to be discovered."*
Lands of Exile: Kith 'n' Kin

CONTENTS

THE DARK VIRGIN REVISITED

"The nails in the tree stump have gone.
The church is ready for a funeral...
There is a bier in the chancel.
No one is around.
The porch is tidier somehow...
The place feels good.

And there are colours now...
Rainbow colours...

As I come out,
A Red-Kite flies
Left to right across the graveyard...

Another bird wheels in low...
And then another...

Oh Don, they are just beautiful.

Whatever has changed the place,
It is incredible..."

Chapter One

BEAN-STALKER

"We are born into perfection."
"And can grow into its reflection."

Broken Crown

7

"You have seen something?" said Pwll.

"O Noble Head," said one of the hog-guards.
"We have seen a forest on the deep, in a place
where we never before saw a single tree."

"And there was a mountain close to that forest,"
said another of the hog-guards.

"With dark ridges near its summit," said a third.

"And just below those ridges, two lakes,"
said the first hog-guard.

"And the surfaces of those lakes were
leaping and jumping wildly," said the second.

"For they were stirred by a great and terrible wind,"
finished the third hog-guard.

"That is indeed a strange sight," said Pwll.
"What does it mean?"
Crucible of the Sun.

Anu has been staring up at the Ball of Power for the last ten minutes.

He attributes to the Ball of Power magic in the form of independent movement, which it simply does not possess. Every so often he glances at me and then back at the Ball of Power.

He knows that I hold the key to this independent movement. He cannot see that this makes the movement dependant on me.

"It's just a ball Anu."

"He thinks it's a bird. He's a bird dog."

This bald statement conjures a picture of a bird-headed dog in my mind, closely followed by a dog-headed bird, immediately followed by the question, which suits Anu the best?

"You're not a bird Anu... you're a dog!"

Anu looks from me to the Ball of Power and back again, then starts to whine, or 'sing' as Wen calls it.

I rise and stand and start to walk over to the Ball of Power...

All Hell breaks loose.

Crisis!

The Milk Cow has finished giving... Akin to a second weaning but worse... this is a call to arms.

"Go forth, young man, and make your way in the world," says Mum.

Jacques is anything but worldly. He believes in magic. He believes to such an extent that he is willing to give everything he has in return for five beans... magical.

Mum knows better and now she has her answer...

""Five beans... magical?" Bah!" Jacques will never amount to anything, so she casts the beans aside without a second thought and banishes him to the attic supperless and badly beaten.

Jacques' tears of pain at his worthlessness activate the beans in the night and in the morning a stalk stands proud in the ground outside his window, yoking Earth and Heaven.

"Up the stalk then, young Jacques my lad, and see what you can find."

"As if it were not enough to have yoked the two spheres," mutters Jacques, but secretly he is thrilled that his 'faith' has paid such dividends.

Heaven turns out to be just like Earth only everything is bigger.

At the top of the stalk is a Big Woman.

9

'Mum', Jacques calls her, cleverly, and then plays helpless, asking for food. Like all 'mums' everywhere she is only too happy to oblige the little fellow. She leads Jacques into the kitchen, perhaps thinking he will grow to be as big as her own man who eats everything... including young men.

"Quick, he's coming!" cries the Big Woman, as the Heavenly Ground starts to shake. "Into the cooking pot, he'll never think to look in there."

"Fee Fie Foh Fum," says the Big Fella.
"I smell the Blood of an earth-bound 'un.
If he be living, or if he be dead,
his bones I'll grind to make my bread..."

He does not think to look in the cooking pot for food though and after consuming what is put before him, he falls asleep whilst counting his gold pieces and begins to snore.

In a flash, Jacques is out the cooking pot and out the door, hurtling back down the stalk with the gold pieces.

Mum is pleased, but just like the milk, the gold pieces soon run out. Now what?

Jacques climbs back up the stalk to see what else he can find...

This time the Big Woman is a bit suspicious.

"Do you know anything about missing gold?" she asks.

"I do actually," says Jacques, as the ground starts to shake again. "Keep me safe and I'll tell you where it is."

So the Big Woman puts Jacques in the oven. "He'll never think to look in here."

"Fee Fie Foh Fum," says the Big Fella.
"I smell the Soul of an earth-bound 'un.
If he be free, or if he be caught,
his flesh I'll have to nourish my heart."

He does not think to look in the oven for food though and after consuming what is put before him, he falls asleep whilst petting his golden-egg-laying hen and begins to snore.

In a flash, Jacques is out the oven and out the door, hurtling back down the stalk with the golden-egg-laying hen.

Mum is pleased, the golden eggs never run out but the hen eventually dies. Now what?

Jacques climbs back up the stalk to see what else he can find. This time Jacques waits until the Big Woman goes out then sneaks into the kitchen just as the ground begins to shake. He leaps into the copper and pulls the lid over himself thinking, "He'll never think to look in here."

"Fee Fie Foh Fum," says the Big Fella.
"I smell the Spirit of an earth-bound 'un.
If he be moving, or if he be still,
I'll take a draught and drink my fill..."

He does not think to look in the copper for sustenance though and after consuming what was left out for him he falls asleep listening to his self-playing harp and starts to snore. In a flash, Jacques is out the copper and out the door and hurtling back down the stalk with the self-playing harp...

...But the harp calls out to its master. "Wake up, wake up! The earth-bound lad is stealing away with me."

So the Big Fella wakes up. Quick as a flash, he comes charging down the stalk after Jacques. But Jacques is too quick and Jacques is too nimble and he reaches the earth before the Giant. He takes an axe to the bean-stalk, so that it comes crashing down with the Big Fella still clinging to it... and in the fall, he breaks his crown.

"What?"

11

"I don't know what you mean."

"You're looking at me funny."

"It's a fairy tale, Don..."

"I thought you liked fairies?"

"I do but... well, it's hardly School specific, is it?"

"It is too!"

"How is it School specific?"

"The Milk-Cow is the Soul-Call... the outer no longer sustains."

"Mmmm..."

"Mmmm... metanoia."

"Mmmm... movement up?"

"Movement up is movement in."

"If movement up is movement in, then movement down is movement out... and the Giant is?"

"The Giant is all the centres in turn because psychologically..."

"...All the centres are giants. But what about the treasures?"

"The treasures are abilities of the soul which assure success in life and continuation beyond. They ascend correspondingly with each foray and as each 'higher', or 'deeper' realm is successfully traversed."

Wen is still worried about the insanity of it all, but fairy stories only appear insane to us now because we have become so separated from truth. As children, we accepted their subconscious logic intuitively. It both satisfied our sense of justice in the developing weirdness of the world around us and reassured us that all would eventually be well again... in fact, was still well, even though it did not necessarily appear that way.

"All the great thinkers recognise the importance of rational thought and also the importance of getting beyond the rational and that's where the myths and fairy stories come in. Plato spends the greater part of his master work, *The Republic*, berating the poets and story-tellers for telling lies in their myths and then he ends his opus with... a myth.'

"Well, to err is human... But no one's going to read a book in which all the characters are giants."

"Yet we all live in a world dictated by them. But perhaps you're right... they have become something of an obsession. The more self-remembering I do, the more giant-like my body and everyone else's body seems to become. And they do make an appearance in all the mythological traditions... the Titans, the Jotunn, the Asuras, the Fomoire... usually as opponents of the gods, that have to be overcome, subdued and then kept at bay, lest the heaven world be breached and fall."

Wen becomes pensive for a while. "We need to go to Cerne Abbas."

"Father Corn?"

"Possibly. And then there's the Long Man of Wilmington, whose 'long man' is no longer visible and of course, Gogmagog..."

"Atta girl! I'm thinking these are all chalk figures?"

"They were all hill figures once, though Gogmagog no longer exists. But he was also a rock and was later split in two and represented in the stonework of cathedrals and other media, like the wicker-work figures carried at the Lord Mayor's show for one. The 'gianting' traditions of our country, and others in Europe for that matter, are still very much alive and kicking and that's even before we start to consider the biblical references..."

"The giants are right up our street then, so to speak. Or a street nearby. When do we start?"

"I think we already have," smiles Wen. "You know the Long Man of Wilmington is an Opener, or that's one interpretation of his stance, but the 'door jambs' could also be staves, or sight-lines."

"In which case, the Long-Man is a Dod-Man and responsible for marking out the Leys."

"We still don't really know what the ley energies actually are."

"On the contrary, my dearest Wendolina. I know *precisely* what those energies are."

"Can you wait while I swallow this mouthful of food before telling me?"

"Your faith in me is most reassuring! But you will like this. Are you ready now?"

13

"Uhuh. Ready."

"The Ley-Lines are Cause-Ways."

"You're right. I do like that. Where's it from?"

"It's from the Myth of the Green Harper..."

THE GREEN HARPER

"Peedy Weedy
Pally Ludy
Lady Whistle
Lody Wassel
and Great Big Hodyman Dod..."
Traditional Toe Counting Rhyme.

"When I was little, "Peedy Weedy" was a little piggy that went to market, "Pally Ludy" stayed at home, "Lady Whistle" ate roast beef, "Lody Wassel" had none, and Great Big Hodyman Dod, well, he went, "pee wee-wee- wee-wee... all the way home.""

"That's pretty much what happened when I was little too, although in a slightly different order. Interesting though, don't you think, the emphasis on polarity?"

"Yes, and also the emphasis on bodily maintenance."

"But it does seem to imply that it is possible to walk home."

"So, how do we get back home?"

"By walking the earth."

Big-Boss Stud was a crafty fellow.
He held sway over the whole of Albion.

His magic saw to the weather,
and his magic saw to the harvest.
His magic was good.

14

He lived in Mercia and had the measure
of all the fair-mounds
and game-plains in the country...

"Fair-mounds?"

"We'd probably call them hillforts now."

"Game-plains?"

"As in hunting game."

"Okay, let me get this straight. Everything that was not a fair-mound was a game-plain?"

"Correct."

"And everything that was not on a fair-mound... was fair-game?"

"Also correct."

"Including humans?"

"You're getting good at this."

Now, Elkmar and Aini built a house on the bank of the river Avon.

Aini had the form of a great white cow but she also had the form of a fair and beautiful woman.

Big-Boss Stud wanted to sleep with her.

Aini was amenable to that but she feared the power and the might of Elkmar, for his whiskers were tough and his tusks were long.

"Why the form of a cow and a woman?"

"It's a way of recognising the relationship of the worlds."

"But to what end?"

"Understanding."

"But I don't think I do. Understand... I mean."

"The easiest one to grasp is the Sun-Ray-Corn-Earth equivalence."

"The Sun, Ray, Corn, Earth equivalence? Oh! I think I've got it! The corn sprouts from the earth like rays of light shine out from the sun."

"And in drawing that equivalence, you're recognising a universal process. I told you it was an easy one. No less beautiful for that though. We can probably go further by saying the stalks of corn are the rays of light from the Sun-Field projected through the Earth-Field."

"Projected through what?"

"A particular seed... and the right conditions."

"Neat."

"Can you think of any other equivalencies? Animal ones, perhaps?"

"But of course. The Sun is a Horse, the Moon is a Cow."

"...and the Earth?"

"The Earth is a Sow!"

"Why is the Sun a Horse?"

"Because it carries each of us to other worlds."

"Why is the Moon a Cow?"

"Because it sustains us in the shadow of the Earth."

"And why is the Earth a Sow?"

"Because of its prodigious progeny."

"I think you're right on all counts but I think they took it further. Can you express all that qualitatively?"

"I think so. How about... the Sun is a Horse, for Generation. The Moon is a Cow, for Dispensation. And the Earth... the Earth is a Sow, for Recompense."

"Perfect! It's all in there in a succinct form which has to be thought about in order to yield its meaning... just like the myth itself."

"Or just like a seed."

❖

16

So Big-Boss Stud sent Elkmar on an errand to Ekane, his beautiful son by Elatha, in the Plain of Fair Isles.

"Whatever task I am set," said Elkmar, "I will accomplish it in the space of one whole night and one whole day and I shall be back with Aini before evening."

"You must build a system of Cause-Ways to link these isles one to the other," said Ekane.

"No easy task that," said Elkmar, "but I am the equal of it." And he called to him his flocks, and his herds.

But Big-Boss Stud, had already put three crafty spells of magic on him, so that Elkmar felt no hunger and he felt no thirst and he saw no sun set for the space of nine full moons, which passage of time seemed to him but the length of one whole night, and one whole day, during which time he and all his people, worked at the task which Ekane had set him, and to right good effect at that!

"The Plain-of-Fair-Isles?"

"Is a slightly different conception of the fair-mound and game-plain which draws them together and makes of them a different level."

"One that is more malleable, perhaps?"

"One that has the potential for more malleability, certainly."

"The system of Cause-Ways... are Ley-Lines?"

"The energies of each 'Isle' flow between each other as cause and effect. Those that are traversable are designated High-Ways with the same status and protection as the fair-mounds."

"Hence the traditional sanctity of the highways."

"The innkeepers on the High-Ways were sort of priests, offering sanctuary and succour as a service to travellers of the way."

"Way-farers!"

"Isn't it wonderful how the ideas are still contained in the language?"

"They're just sort of waiting to pop out."

17

"Into a cognisance which yields understanding..."

It was in this way that Big-Boss Stud managed to sleep with Aini; and he lived with her in her house on the bank of the river Avon for nine full turns of the moon, while the child of their union grew in her womb.

When Aini was about to give birth, Big-Boss Stud called for his harp so that he might smooth the pangs of the child's passage with his music...

"Nine fillings of the moon?"

"The nine personality types."

"As much of the perfection of the sun light as each month can hold."

"Nobody is born perfect."

"Nobody grows perfect."

"But we are born into perfection."

"And can grow into its reflection."

A fair harper of melodious art was Big-Boss Stud, and although, at first, his music was sad and mournful to reflect the travails of Aini's labour, it soon became joyful and happy at the birth, and then quiet and peaceful as Aini fell into a deep, heavy sleep...

When Aini awoke from her slumber, Big-Boss Stud was holding their child.

"You must receive your son, O Passionate One," he said, "and forever shall the music of sorrow and laughter and sleep be heard when the women of Albion bring forth their young."

Aini took the child in her arms.

"He shall be called Aeth," she said, "for only one who shines with the brightness of the Day-Fire could be conceived after dusk and born before dawn."

And then she laughed out loud and smiled on her son...

"All of this was accomplished outside of time?"

"It had to be, lest Elkmar discover the ruse."

"So a new system of communication and trade was established, simply in order to allow the god-like energies to have congress."

"That's one way of looking at it."

"A sort of object lesson in reciprocal relations."

"Sort of, but there were other repercussions of the ruse."

"The tale continues? What happens next?"

"All in good time, sweet Gwendoline..."

I have been worrying about Anu.

Playing fetch all day, every day cannot be much fun.

Even for a bird-dog...

...or a dog-bird...

...or whatever he is.

Whatever he is, he must be able to read minds, because the next time I visit Wen, I notice that he has introduced a new component to his game of fetch.

Instead of dropping the Ball of Power at my feet on his return, he now trots around the dining table and drops it so that it rolls under the table where I cannot see it.

Hide and Seek!

He has obviously been worried about me.

"Playing fetch all day, every day cannot be much fun.

19

Even for a Bird-Man...

...or a Man-Bird..."

...or whatever it is that I am.

"I don't even know where Cerne Abbas is."

"It's in Dorset."

"Is Set's Door near Devon?"

Wen pauses for a moment and then smiles. "Yes. If Cornwall is the toe of the foot of the country, then Devon is the ball of the foot of the country and Dorset is the arch of the foot of the country."

I am very much enjoying this description of the place names of Albion. It makes it sound like the country has got a giant club foot.

"Albion *was* a giant originally," smiles Wen, unfolding a map of the ancient country. "Look, in those days Dorset was the domain of the Durotriges clan."

"Wow! Where did you get this?"

"Map shop?"

I am not sure I believe her. It is much more likely that this has fallen from heaven like manna of old. It has all the ancient sites marked on it and *everything*. It is a vocational moment. The world has finally changed for the better and now... anything can happen!

"You know this means that the heel of the foot of the country is called Dover?"

"Yeahhs," says Wen, eyeing me with suspicion. She knows me too well already.

"Well, that makes Albion fleet-footed, like Mercury. Albion's heels are Dove winged!"

Chapter Two
GIANTS, GIANTS, EVERYWHERE!

Breakfast in Slug Town...

Big Nick

"That forest, O Noble Head," said Amech-the-Herb,
"is the masts of the ships and their yards,
in the fleet assembled by Tyrnonos
to avenge the 'rape' of his mistress.
The mountain is Tyrnonos' might,
its dark ridges the furrowed brow of his anger,
and the two lakes are the tears of his grief
at the loss of his son."
She continued, looking out from the rock,
far and wide over the horizon,
"Stirred by his rage,
he is impelled across the water to Annwn
to assuage the loss that he has suffered
and to retrieve his son."
Crucible of the Sun

I feel I ought to explain...

We were supposed to be going to Scotland. But Wen made the coffee pot 'explode' and so we could not really go anywhere till all the bandages were off.

"Don! I did not *make* the coffee pot explode!"

"So what happened?"

"I was in the kitchen..."

"Alone?"

"...I was in the kitchen, alone, plunging the plunger of the cafetière, as I have done a thousand times before without any problem. Only this time... it got jammed half way down. And then coffee, just sort of... went everywhere."

"The coffee, of its own volition, just "sort of went everywhere?""

"It was an accident."

Accident or no... we could not go... to Scort-land.

22

Which in some ways, Wen's injuries, (which were quite severe) notwithstanding, did turn out to be something of, if not a blessing in disguise exactly, then 'not quite such a downer as at first supposed'.

We did, in any case, have a bit of mopping up to do after our last little adventure.

A re-read of Watkins threw up a possible reason for the apparently special qualities of Our Rainbow Chapel and, in order to follow that lead, we decided to trip along to churches in Windsor... and Stowe... and North Marston, all of which were apparently on the same line.

And we had wanted to visit the barrows at Ivinghoe for some time but had not yet had the opportunity. Again, according to Watkins, Ivinghoe was a Beacon Hill and also on a ley... which when we checked... arrowed straight and true... through ORC.

"Did Scott get Ivanhoe from Ivinghoe?"
"I shouldn't think so. Scott was... well erm, Scottish."
"Ha, ha, ha..."
"Did you do that on purpose?"

Then Wen really got her eye in and started mapping a lot of the other churches we had tapped and sure enough we now have three lines of churches... all centred on ORC.

We also wanted to spend some more time in the churches that we 'raided' last time out, so St Lawrence's at Broughton and Chalfont St Giles' also needed to be revisited and firmed up.

Our little vacation was already looking like the proposal of some manic busman and that was even before Wen's spectral announcement about Cerne Abbas... which did have the ring of something that simply had to be obeyed.

To that end, I arranged to travel down on a Saturday afternoon so we could take a more leisurely look at St Lawrence's of Broughton... and we were not disappointed...

❖

"Doom's wall..."

The wall of Doom...

It gave us the key to the 'floating head' syndrome.

It showed us the righteous as angelic winged heads.

And the Maw of Hell, was merely the gaping mouth of a giant swallowing people whole.

It also appeared to depict an angel with a rather large sword dressed as a Jester but then, the less said about that the better... for now at least.

There was also an intriguing Pietà, depicting the effect of blasphemy upon the 'body' of Christ. The various blasphemers are shown coveting the parts of the Christ's body which their calumnies have torn asunder. Needless to say, there are fourteen such miscreants and if the Doom in some respects reminds us of the Egyptian 'weighing of the heart', then this scene cannot but remind us of the dismembered Osiris.

Interesting, when one considers that at the time these walls were painted, to all intents and purposes, nobody was supposed to have heard of either the weighing of the heart or the dismemberment of Osiris...

I need to stress this word 'leisurely'.

What I have in mind here, if you can picture it, is the slow, easy drift of a barge making its way down an English canal...

This is the optimum speed of movement on a vacation.

It is a speed at which events unfold in their own good time without undue or unnatural force.

It is akin to the breathing of the universe.

If you contrast this with the speeding bullets which whine up and down the motorways on a daily basis, you will begin to understand why so many of us are lost.

We are moving too quickly to see anything. And those things we do catch glimpses of, are supplanted too quickly by others before reflection has even begun to set in, let alone been anywhere near accomplished.

"It is good, my dearest Gwendolina, that you are so interested in this word 'leisurely'..."

"I'm not sure that I am all that interested, actually."

"...for I am a past master in its operations. My leisurely breakfasts, on a good day, can stretch well into the afternoon. Which, pretty much, makes lunch supper... which is fine by me, for, as you know, I am of the considered opinion that we eat far too much anyway."

Wen does not really 'get' leisurely.

She is a bouncing ball of energy that never sleeps... though that may be due to all the coffee...

Maybe that is what the coffee was trying to tell her when it exploded?

Slow down a bit.

If it was, then it is not the first time recently that this advice has been given.

I do hope she starts to pay heed soon.

I, on the other hand, probably need to speed up... a bit.

Jack Sprat and all that.

"And all this talk of bits..."

"Yeahhs?"

"It reminds me of another of Albion's Myths."

"Oh Don! Which one?"

"Aha! So now that I've finally got your attention..."

25

BREAKFAST IN SLUG TOWN

"Slug Town?"

"A slug is a bullet and a bullet is a speeding car, remember?"

"A slug is also a slimy pest that destroys crops."

"Ah, but the name slug contains lug and Lug is a god of light."

"I thought that was Lugh. And I thought he was Irish."

"It is also Lugh, and 'he' is 'Irish' now but 'he' must also have once been in Albion because we have Lugdunum which is London, (or is it Lyon, I can never remember, probably on the same line which would lead us back to Albion anyway because of Lyonesse, and Lugh too, because only the Lion with a steady hand can catch the sun and..."

"And what?"

"...and hold it steady enough to eat it,) and then there's Ludgate, which definitely *is* in London and Luton which is near London and Leicester..."

"...which is nowhere near London and which doesn't sound that much like Lug either..."

"...which is indeed nowhere near London but which was once spelled Leycester... Because there was once a Lord of that name and the Lords of the land, as everyone in their right mind knows, rape the land and take its name, and that could be linked to London by a line of light too because Lug is light like Luke... and well like 'like' too actually and also like Lux and Luc and so if we are lucky it could be linked to a topic which is very dear to our hearts..."

"..!"

"...and which is today, with its change in spelling to Leicester, quite indisputably a town of leisure or luxury, so that what we have here, perhaps, in Slug Town, is a place of fast-slow or slow-fast... or fast-slow... slow-slow-fast... shall we dance?"

"Don, you really are insane!"

"Incidentally, the reason why to refrain from food is called a fast is because it makes time go quicker... it makes time go... fast, in fact. I thought you wanted to be a Filid? Lucky for you that you found me if you do... A slug is also a draught of liquid and together, my dear apprentice of insanity, we can slurp in the slug-light. I mean, even their slimy trails look like solidified light... Blimey! Solidified, slimy slug trails could be the lines of light we call leys... if only they were straight..."

"Is this what they did? The Filidh?"

"Sort of. It doesn't work quite so well in English. Well, strictly speaking it doesn't work at all in English, but in the Gaelic language the vowels and the consonants mutate and merge and skip around dancing from word to word and the master Filidh were masters of pronunciation and gave life to it all in that way... by sounding..."

"Sound!"

"Quite. Do you realise that the word 'silent' and the word 'listen' are comprised of the same set of letters, arranged in a different order?"

"And what can be gained from listening to the silence I wonder?"

"Well, nothing actually because you can't listen *to* silence, you have to listen *in* silence. Try it!"

❖

27

... No smoke from the roof-rounds
of Albion without tribute to them...

A tribute on the Quern
A tribute on the Kneading Trough
A tribute on the Baking Flags

An ounce of gold for every nose
North, South, East or West of
the Wondrous Head...
The Annals of Albion.

"The roof-rounds?"

"Roundhouses... the doorway aligned to the rising sun... a smoke hole in the centre of the roof. It really is the only way to live."

"Quern?"

"A hand held grinding mill for corn."

"Cerne?"

"Interesting isn't it? Does it refer to the raised club in the Giant's hand? There are plenty of other more popular theories and it is a rather large club to be used for grinding corn. Were the ancients of that time subtle enough to make a play on the raising of the bread and the raising of the member? Or even on the killing of the living and on the raising of the dead. There are many who doubt it. And it is true that from our perspective, there are a host of other more obvious analogies."

"Host? Oh Don, stop it."

"A host is something or someone who receives someone or something..."

"It can also be an army."

"And an army is a body which receives the fighting force is it not?"

"*Okaayy*... but it may be that it comprises a fighting force."

"It is prised from the company, certainly. But you're right, the bread and the hotelier are more interesting because they highlight the

28

nature of the something or someone as a guest."

"In the case of the bread, as a divine guest."

"In the case of the hotelier too, perhaps."

"Explain..."

"Every other is divine, especially a guest."

"Why 'especially' a guest."

"Because that is the divine, recognised and welcomed into your domain and at your disposal."

"A sacred contract..."

"...which it is sacrilege to break."

"And the fighting force?"

"Mars was once considered a God was it not?"

"He was..."

"An ounce of gold?"

"Ah... the original Poll Tax. Politicians beware... This NEVER works. As we shall hopefully see during the course of this story. And it does not matter how you try to disguise it. This NEVER works."

When the slug-men took Albion, they put the whole of that green land under tribute and the Champions of the crafty folk were made vassals of the slug king, Grim-Gaze.

Father Fish had a house in Eden Dale and he was employed constructing earthworks and ramparts for the new slug town which was to be built there. He was very unhappy in his work and was forced to share his table with an idle churl called Gob-Gut.

Gob-Gut considered his own meal small and Father Fish's large so he said, "Father Fish, my housekeeping is bad tonight, for the sake of your honour let the three best bits of your serving be given to me."

And so every night Father Fish would give Gob-Gut three large bits from his serving which were each the size of a small pig.

Now these three bits comprised a third of Father Fish's supper and he began to look the worse for the loss of them.

❖

"Who are the Crafty-Folk?"

"Who are they indeed? Or what are they? According to the tradition they are the most handsome and delightful company. With the fairest form. The most distinguished in their skill... with music... and playing... The most gifted of mind and temperament... And the company that, although the bravest, also inspired the most horror, fear and dread. Apparently, they excelled all the people of the world at large with their proficiency of every art."

"Wow! They just sound so neat!"

"Don't they just..."

"Slug-Men?"

"The Fomoire... or the 'For More'... Everything they do is designed for more. They have this much food... they want to get this much more... insatiable desire... They're the giants... a giant, by definition, has no discrimination... that's why it grows so large."

"Giant Slugs... ugh! As such you'd think they'd be able to build their own earthworks."

"Except, they're not able to build anything at all, they only consume or destroy what's already there."

"Okay... Earthworks and ramparts?"

"Henges and mounds and the means by which to enter them."

"Which part of a ram allows entry to a fair-mound?"

"A most noble question, sweet Gwen, to which the answer can only be, that part which spirals."

"The Horns!"

"Which are used both for drinking and also sounding."

"If three bits of Father Fish's meal comprises a third, his whole meal must comprise... nine bits."

"Sounded, like a true Filid... and as every true Filid knows, wholemeal is better than no meal."

❖

30

One fine day Father Fish was working in a trench when he saw Little Nipper coming toward him.

Said Little Nipper, "Well then, Father Fish?"

"Indeed, I am well," said Father Fish.

"So what makes you look so bad?" asked Little Nipper.

Replied Father Fish, "Every-night at supper Gob-Gut the slug-man demands from me the three best bits of my serving."

"A bad situation and no mistake," said Little Nipper, "but here, I have some advice for you," and he put his hand into his purse, and took out three gold pieces which he gave to Father Fish. "Put one gold piece into each of the three bits for Gob-Gut and they will stick in his throat and he will choke."

Father Fish put the three gold pieces in his pocket, "'T will be a warm night in Eden Dale, and my thanks to you, if you're right," he said, and then he rubbed his belly...

"What?"

"Are there any horns sounding yet?"

"Well, I'm enjoying it if that's what you mean?"

"St Nicholas."

"St Nicholas?"

"The three bags of gold with which he saved the prostitutes by giving them as a dowry."

"No!"

"Why not? Father Fish is being prostituted."

"Three gold pieces... which become three gold balls on the pawnbroker's sign... and more prostitution."

"The very same."

Now, when Father Fish was walking home from work that

31

evening he met a woman washing in a burn. She had one foot on the south bank of the burn and the other foot on its northern bank.

A good looking young woman she was, with a fine figure and hair that hung loose in nine beautiful tresses which swished, first one way, and then the other, as she washed herself. Father Fish desired her greatly so they talked together.

"By the nine rivers of Albion," said Father Fish, "you are a fine woman."

"And you are a grand big man," replied the woman, and then she smiled at him.

"You are a witch," said Father Fish, stepping into the burn.

"And you are bewitched," she laughed, splashing him with water...

"Okay. So St Nicholas is now turning in his grave."

"Not necessarily."

"Huh?"

"Don't you think that a man who went out of his way to prevent the prostitution of souls would quite readily approve of a contract, any contract undertaken by mutual consent?"

"Well, when you put it like that..."

Now that woman's name was Grey-Sway, and she agreed to meet Father Fish at his house in Eden Dale on the following night.

As Father Fish continued on his way home he fingered the three gold pieces in his pocket, thinking, "Why, 'tis the luck on me already!"

"All Father Fish's X-masses have come at once!"

"Well not quite yet awhile but that is definitely the spirit..."

So that evening, Father Fish did as he was bid by Little Nipper and sure enough, Gob-Gut choked to death on the three best bits of his serving.

Now the slug-men at once went to their king and said, "Father Fish has killed Gob-Gut with a poisonous herb."

It was for this reason that Grim-Gaze, king of the slug-men, sanctioned the execution of Father Fish...

"Oh!"

Said Father Fish, "Your decree is most unjust. Gob-Gut was forever demanding the three best bits of my serving and I was beginning to look the worse for it. So last night I placed three gold pieces in my supper for luck, but when Gob-Gut asked for the three best bits why, I had to give him those that contained the gold and he died from them."

King Grim-Gaze ordered the body of Gob-Gut cut open and on finding the three gold pieces he commuted Father Fish's sentence.

Instead of killing Father Fish outright, the slug-men made a fulsome porridge for him. They filled the king's cauldron with eight gallons of milk, and meal, and fat, then they poured the porridge into a hole. Then king Grim-Gaze declared, "Finish the porridge in one sitting and your life will be spared."

So Father Fish took up his ladle. "This is good food if its taste is equal to its smell," he said, setting about the porridge, and after every ladleful he declared, "Aye, 'tis that indeed, and its poor bits do not spoil it."

On eating his fill, he put down the ladle, scraped his bent finger over the mould and gravel in the bottom of the hole and fell asleep.

His belly was now big as a house cauldron and all the slug-men laughed at it...

"Breakfast in Slug Town!"
"Shshsh... This is the best bit of the tale..."

Now, as Father Fish lay in the hole in the ground sleeping off his meal who should happen along but Grey-Sway herself.

She jumped into the hole and landed on his stomach. Father Fish immediately woke up and looked at Grey-Sway angrily.

"What business did you have, woman, falling on me like that."

"This business," said Grey-Sway, "to get you to carry me on your back to my father's house."

"And who might your father be?" asked Father Fish.

"Why, I am the daughter of Grim-Gaze, king of the slug-men."

"In that case," said Father Fish, with a glint in his eye, "I will not carry you upon my back unless you guess my name."

So Grey-Sway began to beat his stomach.

"Get up and carry me on your back, O Big Bellied Man," she said.

Said Father Fish, "That is not my name."

Then she beat his stomach harder saying, "Get up and carry me on your back, O Coarse, Foul Mouthed Warrior."

Said Father Fish, "That indeed is not my name."

Now pummelling his stomach she cried, "Get up and carry me on your back, O Long Limbed Father of the Turning World!"

Said Father Fish, "That name is too much." He emptied his stomach of its contents and filled his trousers with cack. "Woman, you must mock me the less," he said.

"Well, I can but try," said Grey-Sway looking about the hole and pinching her nose, "'though 't will certainly be a hard thing for me."

Father Fish stood up and removed his soiled trousers then he tied his belt around his waist and offered her his back...

"The best bit of the tale?" whispers Wen.

"The best bit of the tail, is the bit that swishes like Grey-Sway's tresses because a swish is a wish in disguise... now shshsh!"

So Grey-Sway jumped astride Father Fish, and with her legs straddling his back and her arms around his neck, she whispered in his ear, "You shall not get to my father's house by any means!"

Said Father Fish, "Why certainly, I will get there!"

"But I shall be a giant oak in every pass you come to," whispered Grey-Sway.

Said Father Fish, "And my axe will make a mark in every oak forever."

"But I shall be a stone at the mouth of every ford you cross," whispered Grey-Sway.

Said Father Fish, "And I will leave the trace of my heel on every stone forever."

So Grey-Sway struck Father Fish on the side to get him moving, and off he went, with his leather cape coming only as far as the hollow of his elbows, and his grey-brown tunic rising up around his rump and exposing his long penis which trailed in the ground and made a trench between his hairy, horse-hide shoes...

"A long penis?"

"Very good!"

"No, I mean, if Father Fish is making the henges with his penis, he must be a giant."

"Didn't I warn you? They're everywhere!"

"Little Nipper?"

"A giant crab. And where would one be likely to find a giant crab?"

"In the sky!"

"Along with the Big Dipper..."

"Which, as well as being a roller coaster, is also a Giant Bear."

"Atta girl!"

On drawing within sight of her house Grey-Sway again whispered in Father Fish's ear, "Here we are at last but you shall never overcome my father, Grim-Gaze."

Said Father Fish, "Why, for sure I shall overcome your father, I will take from him the strength of his heart and the blood of his valour."

At this Grey-Sway jumped down from his back, revealing her pubic hair, and that day Father Fish gained himself a mistress.

The mark where they met remains at Balshaw's Strand.

"Balshaw?"

"Bel's shore..."

"And the Strand?"

"A promontory of land which juts into the sea, basically it's another headland: another conjugal state of landscape from the ancients' point of view."

"But which came first, the experience or the form?"

"Well, as they would have been very much in the landscape, presumably the experience, which was then only later confirmed by observation of the form."

"I am very much reminded of the Aboriginal Dreaming."

"It does seem to be a similar conception of being. Malaga Man he went walking... he walked this way... walking, walking... he got tired here... sat down and fell asleep. Rainbow Snake emerged from a Water-Hole whilst he slept. That snake tried to swallow him whole. Malaga Man woke up in time and caught hold of Rainbow Snake's tail. It broke off in his hands. He dropped it then... left shards of rainbow everywhere."

"One wonders where they are getting it from."

"Then one realises that they're reading it in the land."

"Hmmm... Is that the end?"

"Hardly, it is just the beginning. You seem a little nonplussed?"

"I'm still not totally convinced by the St Nicholas connection."

"Ah, you're just sore because I shushed you."

"I am not! It is a bit tenuous though don't you think?"

"On its own, it would be perhaps, but the ship episode from St Nick's legend is linked too."

"What, the miracle where Nick boards the ship, the crew's food is lost in a storm so they eat the cargo and when they pull in to port the cargo is wholly intact? It is linked to this story, in what way?"

"Not this story, though as it develops you'll see some more parallels. But the character which Father Fish is based on is, in the tradition, reputed to possess a cauldron of plenty. The ship's miraculously replenished cargo is merely a later version of the same concept."

"Well, I'll give you that, I suppose, and reserve judgment on the rest."

"My lady is too kind. By the way, he also possesses a rather large club."

Wen smiles but says nothing...

"The club is knobbed."

Still nothing...

Chapter Three
RAVEN WALK

"…she saw a small field of crystal and semi-precious stones laid out in a spiral pattern on the floor. There were huge clusters of amethyst and quartz, glittering pyrites and all the varied hues of agate. One large stone, polished by the dripping moisture from the stalactites above, looked like black glass, frozen around a snowstorm…"

Ogmios' Garden, "Swords of Destiny"

"Follow me…"

...Now, Hide and Seek, is a very noble game.

In fact it is a divine game. It is a game of the Gods.

The Gods, of course, get to hide because it is always more fun hiding than finding.

Unless, that is, you are a Human, finding a God perhaps...

The Gods hide themselves in the mundane world around us and we have to find them...

I look at Anu trotting around the table like a horse in dressage...

As he is about to drop the Ball of Power from his mouth...

...I begin to wonder *how* he knew about Hide and Seek?

..."I've been thinking about all these giants," said Wen.

"Well it would be difficult not to."

"Maybe we need a big church to contain them."

"A cathedral? Well, we were going to drop in on York Minster before the coffee escapade, remember but then... what are you expecting to find there anyway?"

"Well, if the theory is correct it should contain all the colours but in a greater density and profusion shouldn't it?"

"Possibly, but that photo-shot through Whitchurch window is as good as anything I've seen in printed form about Chartres..."

"Ahh Chartres... when do we get to go to Chartres Don?"

"All in good time... and in any case, it might not work like you suppose. Look at Stonehenge. Most people I know who have visited recently have been devastated, and then there's the Brugh-na-Boyne too, another utter disaster of restoration."

"I remember visiting Stonehenge before there was any fence around it. When you could climb all over the stones, all day and all night if you wanted to..."

"I bet you did too, didn't you?"

"Almost! Not too many of the cathedrals have been too heavily restored though, or at least not to that extent."

"They'll be full of people and I bet you have to pay to go around some of them."

"Well, we pay when we go to our churches."

"I know we do but that is discretionary. It makes such a difference. It's the spirit of the thing."

"You're right."

It is the spirit. That is it exactly. That's what this whole thing is about...

OF TRUTH AND LEGEND

The Silver Well...

Legend says that St Augustine once visited Dorset. While he was there, he met some shepherds grazing their flocks and asked them whether they would prefer beer or water to drink. The temperate shepherds replied 'water' whereupon St. Augustine struck the ground with his staff, crying, 'Cerno El' as the water gushed out. The words were supposedly a pun on Cernel, the old name of the village and meant 'I perceive God.'

Today it is thought that the legend was probably invented by the Benedictine monks of Cerne Abbey to serve as an attraction to pilgrims.

Closer to the truth perhaps is the story of St. Edwold, a member of the Mercian Royal Family who one day had a vision of a silver well.

He went wandering through the countryside and when he came to Cerne he gave some silver pennies to a shepherd in return for bread and water. The shepherd then showed him a well where he could drink and St Edwold recognised it as the well of his vision. He built a small hermitage by the spring and lived there until his death in 871...'

Information Plaque, Cerne Abbas

"So how did they know?"

"How did who know what?"

"The Mediaeval artists responsible for the wall paintings at Broughton St Lawrence. How did they know about the weighing of the heart and the dismemberment of Osiris?"

"The 'underground stream'."

"What... it works like the Akashic records, you mean?"

"A little. The underground stream, though, implies a living repository of arcane knowledge. That's one of the things about Mystery Schools. Their sources are mysterious.

"It isn't too different from the symbolism contained in the Tarot cards which surfaced a lot later and to far greater effect, it has to be said.

"What's really interesting is the moralistic spin that has been put on these ideas by the Church Fathers. It is easy for *us* to pick it and in large part dismiss it because we are now familiar with the original concepts and things in that respect have moved on.

"Much less so for the mediaeval peasant or merchant, whose subconscious would respond to the kernel of truth presented in the image and whose mind would then perhaps be more easily swayed by the moralistic overlay."

"And it wasn't just morality."

"All kinds of considerations."

"People have to live."

"Are the monks responsible for the legend of the Silver Well such villains if they tweak the truth in order to entice pilgrims to their shrine? People who have embarked on a pilgrimage always get something, even if that something isn't quite what they bargained for. And how true is the earlier story of St Edwold for that matter. There was doubtless a hermit and a hermitage at one time. How he actually came to be there is quite another matter."

"The Church was sort of like the mediaeval version of television.'"

"And the wall paintings?"

"They were the advertisements."

"Roll up... Roll up... get your morality here..."

"You shouldn't mock Don, it's not all that different to what actually happened when the priests started selling indulgences..."

"O Canny Sisters,
steely eyed, turn the
spindle at your side;
spin a thread for Very-White..."

"Sun and moon
and flowering grass,
love to live yet love to pass;

love's gold and silver flame,
ignites, a world's enchantment
in that name...
Very-White... O Very-White..."

"'tis love I spin for Very-White;
a love which wearies soon,
her beauteous flight, and
quenches it in withering bloom."

"Very-White... O Very-White...
though on this loom is gold and red...
silver, green, and purple thread...
a cowl of black, forever to adorn your head."

"What's that?"

"The Doom of Very-White."

"Not a Doom as in the Dooms on our church walls."

"No, more of a prophecy or fate really but the two concepts are obviously linked."

"By time... if nothing else. Very-White is an odd name."

"It's a transliteration... in the tradition it appears in various forms... Fionnavar... Guinevere... actually, come to think of it, All-White might be better and that would bring in Olwen too..."

"White-Track."

"Does a person with a White Bow follow the White Track more readily I wonder?"

"Why do you ask?"

"Because White-Bow is you, fair Gwendolene. And what is the White Track anyway?"

Wen smiles. "I know where the Doom's from."

"You do?"

"It's the continuation of the Green Harper."

"And how did you work that out?"

"Because it's all about time..."

Wen and I are in the new car which to my untutored eye appears to look like nothing so much as a silver bullet and what is more we are heading down a track which leads... nowhere. At any moment now we are going to find the cul-de-sac and have to turn back.

"Are you sure about this?"

"Sure I'm sure, there's a church down here somewhere, you'll see. It's going to be a little beauty..."

Sometimes I wonder where Wen gets her confidence.

It must be innate. It is clearly not based on anything concrete. We have had a wretched morning 'church tapping' and as we are supposed to be on something of a vacation, and as it is nearing lunchtime... personally, I would far rather we were looking for a nice country inn to hole up at for an hour or so.. Still, she will be right about one thing... if there does happen to be a church at the end of this god forsaken track it will be small.

We have passed about five houses in a quarter of an hour... whether it will be a beauty is another matter altogether, but it will definitely be little. The road opens up suddenly into something of a village green and Wen swings the car violently left and then crunches to a stop on the dry grit.

"Well, you wanted a cathedral!"

Although that is something of an exaggeration and the church is probably not quite big enough to be considered a cathedral, there is not a lot in it.

"Why would anyone want to build a cathedral in the middle of... a field?"

"So they could call it, the Cathedral in the Field, obviously," I smile, indicating the nominal.

"It is old too," says Wen, pointing out the village cross which is in the graveyard of the church. The cross looks Atlantean. Either that or it has been at the bottom of the ocean for a couple of centuries and only recently dredged back up into the cold light of day. One touch and it is sure to disintegrate.

We spy a car park off to the right and head for that.

45

"It really is in a field," says Wen looking out into the expanse of countryside.

My attention has been caught by a solitary red kite spiralling on high. I watch, entranced for a while, as she goes through her repertoire of spectacular air acrobatics which culminates in a sort of half swoop followed by an immediate climb which I have never seen performed before.

"If the avian activity quotient is anything to go by we are in for a treat."

As we turn out of the car park and head for the cathedral my heart sinks. There is some sort of gathering of people in the porch. It is to be sure an odd time and day for a service and perhaps if we are lucky whatever it is may have just finished...

...We are not so lucky for when we get to the gate and read the notice-board it becomes clear that the meditation group are just about to commence their activities. They have each been asked to bring an object which holds meaning for them and they are going to talk a little bit about why. As I am mulling over this idea and coming to the conclusion that it is a good one, one of the women from the group in the porch heads towards the gate in order to discard some water.

Wen, being Wen, pipes up...

"Is the church open today at all?"

"Why yes dear, we'll be starting our little meeting soon but you are welcome to come in and look around, there's plenty of room in there," says the woman and then she laughs. While I am still pondering the reason for the laugh, Wen is bouncing up the pathway, camera at the ready. She looks like a woman on a mission so she has clearly already decided to treat this as another 'raid'.

I run to catch up with her and we crest and pass the porch together, nodding and smiling at the assemblage there who are, it has to be owned, probably as disappointed to see us as we were to see them. They doubtless have us down as spiritual tourists, and in some ways I suppose, and from their point of view, that is what we are. I make a mental note to send the church a gratis copy of the book.

In the event, we do not have too long before the little get together commences and although there is more than enough room inside the huge interior it does feel like some sort of sacrilege to be pottering about the nave whilst they get down to it in the chancel.

We beat a hasty retreat with an armful of brochures and settle down outside on the village cross which thankfully proves to be somewhat sturdier than it looks... It also turns out to be anything but a church cross.

There is a really important point to be made here about perception. Perception is not a passive activity. There is a humungous amount of assumed knowledge making up every single perception that occurs and if we do not have all the information we need, we fill in the blanks from our experience and with what we expect to see and even, in some cases, with what we want to see...

The upright is not a cross at all, in fact if anything it looks more like a Doric column. I merely assumed it was a cross because I had seen so many similar structures before that *were* crosses and also because it is situated in the graveyard of a rather large church. I was expecting to see a cross... so that is what I saw, or rather that is what my mind registered I was seeing.

The thing here is, what would a village cross be called, before it was called a cross. It would, to all intents and purposes, be a phallus and kteis albeit the kteis would be multi-levelled or tri-tiered.

Perhaps the best name for it would be a mark stone... or even... a herm. I ask Wen and she laughs... quite disconcerting that.

"It was always a cross I think, even before they started sculpting the uprights as crosses. They originally stood at cross-roads and were places of exchange and mart around which hamlets and villages eventually grew up; they were though, sometimes also known as 'preaching' stones, and in some places as 'butter' stones too."

"Ah... cross-roads... Thanks, Wen." So actually, my herm was not such a bad guess, although herms are purely masculine whereas these structures appear to be both masculine and feminine.

I start to wonder how many people before me have made the

same sort of assumptions and 'seen' the same thing... and let me be quite specific here, 'seen' something that is not there and not seen something that is there...

Of course the cross no longer stands on a cross-roads and it being so closely associated with the church it really ought to have had a cross. If you look closely there is a metal bracket two thirds the way up the shaft of the upright which may once have held a stone cross beam, although it is also clear that this was not part of the original design because where the metal bracket has been attached the upright has fractured... or maybe the bracket was put there to support the crack... who knows what they got up to in Atlantis...

And then I start to wonder whether we have quite inadvertently discovered the reason for the size of the church. The church is so big simply to hide in plain view the cross which is no longer a cross.

The church is big in order to hide the Congress Stone. It reminds me of something...

"Why is the sky so big?"

"...So that the rain falls in drops."

There is no rain here today though.

Nor is there likely to be any.

It is a stunningly beautiful summer's day, and the drone of the vicar's opening oration and the congregation's responses are still audible from our perch on the steps of the cross which is, in my mind, no longer a cross.

The actual words are not discernible and the service melts quite naturally into the lazy hum of the bees and the skittish activity of the flies... and fluttering butter...

...At some point in the service it seems there is a lone female voice singing in Latin and I was certainly not expecting to hear that kind of an utterance in this day and age...

I become engrossed in the literature from the church. There is apparently an original set of mediaeval windows depicting the life of St Nicholas... and I assume that was what Wen spent the whole time in there snapping from more angles than I knew actually existed in space.

There is also a miraculous stain which has assumed the form of the Virgin and which no amount of drying or white-washing will remove. Wen is busy checking her snaps and I rest the back of my head on the non-cross... and close my eyes... musing on what I have just read...

Before we know it dusk creeps over our little repose...

...It is now silent in the village save for the day's departing birdsong which seemingly mingles so easily with the bright shards of other times... in a jumble... and tumble... and admixture of knowledge, memory, and imagination... of handfastings and contracts, trade and laughter, animals, people, faces, babies, and grandmothers...

And then...

The cold glint of steel... and voices shouting... distant screams... a musket shot and the smell of powder... Sounds of breaking glass... shards reflecting in the light of the fire...

I run into the church...

Jewelled fragments of the holy story are scattered everywhere... a soldier raises a pike to smash a window... Pane by pane, one by one, they are broken, lost to memory and tomorrow's eyes.

Another musket shot, coarse laughter... I hide behind the corner of the tower room...

Three leave the nave, laughing...

Only one now remains...

The one left to finish the destruction...

He stands back, removing his helmet. He looks around. He is uneasy. He is young...

They have gone. I look around. I am uneasy with this... it is still a sacred place, even though I do not like the trappings of wealth here. The Church is greedy and corrupt...but the faith of the people? Should they not be thought of in this? This is their holy place...

I look up at the glowing crimson of the window... an artist's hand made it. It tells of all the virtues I admire... and my mother named me Nicholas...

I do not like this.

I think of my mother, her eyes, seeing her watching me...

Half the window is gone.

My father was a seafarer, long gone now, Nicholas was his favourite saint.

I stand away, and see my mother's eyes again, filled with tears...

I see er.

Standing in the corner..

Watching me. Love and sadness... My Mother... His Mother... All Mothers...

I feel shamed, saddened. Surely God does not need us to decide how He is worshipped?

She watches me from the shadows by the altar...

I cannot look...

My pike is the spear in His side...

From my alcove I see the young soldier break down in tears.

He throws the pike from him and runs from the church.

Little remains.

But the shadow on the wall seems to smile through her tears.

A HOUSE ON THE RIVER

"The 'river' is 'time' isn't it?"

"Why is the river time?"

"Heraclitus."

"You are going to have to expand for those without a background in Greek Philosophy."

"One cannot step into the same river twice because the water of the river has flowed on... because the water of the river is forever flowing on... like time..."

"If time flies... and time crawls... is time an insect... a mere product of the Fall?"

"An insect?"

"In... 'sect.' It's a different order of being, a stepping down. In the tradition, the 'gods' are always assuming the form of insects, or grubs, being swallowed, and consequently... reborn. If by some freak environmental catastrophe the animal world were wiped out tomorrow you can be certain the insects would survive."

"That's probably why there's no stricture on killing them."

51

"And that perfectly absolves my guilt from all the childhood ants I so cruelly crushed, thank you."

"You are welcome, my child. The River bank?"

"...Is outside time."

One of Wen's most recent innovations when we are 'church tapping' is to check out the reading matter. The Bibles in these places are so huge they are invariably left open on the lectern and also invariably the passage from the current reading is marked.

We have had in our time, shall we say, some instructive coincidences.

It is not difficult to see how this could work as a form of divination or guidance, perhaps, which is all true divination can ever really be. It is reputedly 'the Word of God' after all, and whatever your take on that particular claim there is indisputably an awful lot of high wisdom within its pages.

One of the most instructive readings was at Stowe.

I like the name Stowe, it has a female pig in it and the church as it turned out was an absolute pig to find and to get to because it is hidden in the grounds of a public school. Only the most dedicated need apply.

Wen, as you no doubt know by now, is extremely dedicated.

The church itself from our point of view was quite disappointing. A couple of recent and quite unusual windows, which may yet find their way into the body of this narrative, had already made our visit worthwhile though... and then Wen found the reading which, in the context of our continuing quest, suddenly made a sort of sense to me for the first time.

It is what is known in the trade as a realisation.

The passage in question was from Luke's version of the Baptism where instead of just getting on with the description of the rite, he treats it in a very circumspect way. He then launches into the whole genealogy of the Christ through all the Patriarchs right back to God... although he

52

does not actually specify Christ as such he does preface the genealogy with the words, "And Jesus himself began to be about thirty years of age, being (as was supposed) the son of Joseph...etc."

I think the "as was supposed" tag refers to the doctrine of the Virgin Birth in which case the genealogy should simply run, "...and God begat Jesus on Mary" should it not?

It is an unfortunate phrase at a crucial part of a particularly important narrative this supposition business and to my mind it presents the Lord Jesus Christ as, or at least makes him sound like, something of a 'bastard' although clearly that is not the evangelist's intent.

There is an easy way out of this conundrum.

Cut the genealogy and just have, "And Jesus himself began to be Christ about thirty years of age being no longer the son of Joseph."

In fact, you could even leave the genealogy in and just insert "but now" before "the son of God" at the end. That way it makes perfect sense and also legitimises the whole story.

There is another much less satisfactory way out of this particular conundrum, which is to suppose that as we are all God's children anyway, we are, technically, all bastards too!

And that would never do.

"Not least, because it is more blasphemy," Wen is eying me tetchily.

"Only for those without eyes and ears..."

"Who are, unfortunately in this day and age as in any other, Legion."

"...No one has seen God at any time, yet those born of the Light of the World do at all times declare its eternal presence."

...Big Boss Stud gave his son to be fostered by Noin in the House of Light on the Plain of Mercia and Aeth was reared there for nine years. Noin kept a playing field which extended for an equal distance in every direction, north, south, east and west and three fifties of the young boys and girls of the men of light played happily together in that field.

But Aeth felt himself superior to the children of light because of Noin's love for him, and his own great beauty and the nobility of his people, and he fell out with Triath, "I have no mind to speak with you," he said, "it angers me that the son of a vassal should play alongside me."

And Triath answered, "It angers me more that a foundling who knows neither his true father nor his true mother should speak to me in such a way."

Then Aeth ran off to Noin in tears at having been so shamed by Triath before all the Children of Light...

There is another version of the genealogy which is given by Matthew in his gospel just prior to the Nativity.

Matthew, however, does not mention God at all, although he does call Jesus the 'Christ', and he makes it clear that the derivation of the Christhood is from Abraham... through David, the slayer of the giant Goliath, who was anointed by Samuel in secret, just prior to the encounter with the Big Fellow... You begin to see, do you not, the importance of the anointing?

"What's the difference between slaying somebody and killing them?"

"In the overall scheme of things, there is no difference at all but I prefer slay because it is much more suggestive."

Wen smiles. "In the self-same way that you prefer beheading to decapitation?"

"In precisely the same way. Would you like to elucidate?"

"Because being resides in the head and decapitation can only lead to the pit of despair."

"And if you carry on like that you'll be heading for Ireland before you know it."

❖

...Now, Matthew is on much firmer ground here because in doing this he effectively squares the new tradition with the old, in so far as Abraham too was anointed, or christened, by Melchisedek and given the sacrament of bread and wine, which Christ re-introduces to a populace turned well away from what, for want of a better phrase, we might call their righteous peace. It is clear that there are twin genealogies at play:

The anointers... Melchisedek... Eli... Samuel... John the Baptist...

The anointed... Abraham... Samuel... David... the Christ...

It is, for certain, intriguingly powerful stuff and I am not at all sure that I am totally comfortable with what it seems to be telling me.

❖

Congress?

55

"Wen."

"Now."

"I know now."

"What do you now know?"

"I know what the Congress Stone represents."

"Oh really, what does the Stone of Congress represent?"

"It represents a column, or a pillar of light, penetrating the three worlds.'"

"And where does the light which penetrates the three worlds come from?"

"It comes from on high..."

Chapter Four
TWIN SUNS

"...Oh Saviour pour upon me thy Spirit of meekness and love,
Annihilate my Selfhood and be thou all my life..."
Jerusalem: The Emanation of the Giant Albion.

Angel of Heaven, Angel of Earth?

Now here is a curious thing.

For the better part of the last four or five months, Wen and I have been trailing around the churches of Buckinghamshire and in some cases beyond, and on many occasions we have come across a representation of for want of a better name we might call, 'the dragon slaying'. In windows and paintings, on murals and tapestries etc. and without exception the slaying has been performed by one of two characters, either St Michael or St George. This being the case it has become customary for us to regard these two characters as interchangeable, leastways where dragon slaying is concerned and very much as representations of the same energy or force.

Not so!

For here, in the little, single-bodied chapel of Crowell, is a window depicting the two characters, their differences meticulously delineated, and each of them is slaying a different dragon!

Why?

I can think of a few reasons to do with hierarchies but what strikes me most about this stunning window is the fact that St George's dragon is coloured blue and green and appears to have been subdued rather than slain, whilst St Michael's dragon is ruby red and is still in its death throes. Or at least that is the reading when moving from the left light to the right light of the window, or if one prefers from high to low.

If one moves from low to high or from the right light of the window to the left light, the story is rather different. Moving this way St George's Dragon appears to be slumbering whilst St Michael's dragon appears to have awoken!

...."There, there," said Noin, "and what's all this?"

"Triath has mocked me," said Aeth, "he has thrown it in my face that I have neither father nor mother, O Noin, tell me if this is so?"

"It is not so," said Noin, "for Big-Boss Stud is your father and your mother is Aini who lives with Elkmar on the banks of the river

Avon."

"Will you come with me then," said Aeth, "that my father may acknowledge me and give me lands, that I may no longer be hidden away and reviled by the Children of the Men of Light?"

"Why, certainly I will go with you," said Noin.

...Wen and I have taken some more time out in the beer garden of the coaching inn of old Aylesbury, now, and perhaps always, known as the King's Head. It may have been inevitable, but we did have to first ascertain whether this type of inn sign referred to heads that had actually been detached or merely to what might better be called busts. The smart money is undoubtedly on the latter and the tradition we feel is not dissimilar to the representations of the monarch's head that appears upon coins of the realm. The reference is to a head of state then, rather than a head in state, or in a state, or even in a basket.

"Don!"

...So Noin set out with Aeth, her fosterling, to speak with Big-Boss Stud, and when they came to the Navel Mound of Mercia, his dwelling place, they found him in assembly.

"What would he like, this son of mine, who has never been here before?" said Big-Boss Stud.

"He would like you to acknowledge him and to give him land," said Noin, "for he feels it unjust that a son of yours should be without land, and you with the measure of all the Fair-Mounds and Game-Plains of Albion."

"A welcome to him for that," said Big-Boss Stud. "He is ever a son of mine, but the land I have in mind for him is already occupied."

"And what land is that?" asked Noin.

"It is the land and dwelling place on the bank of the river Avon," said Big-Boss Stud.

"What advice, then, can you give to the boy," asked Noin.

And Big-Boss Stud unbuckled his sword belt, leant forward and whispered into the ear of Noin...

...I say time out, but really there is no such thing on the quest. These little tête-a-têtes, as well as providing much needed refreshment and sustenance, are crucial in the understanding of what we are doing, where we have been, and where we are going. Things move so rapidly it is otherwise hard, for me at least, to keep up.

It is nice too to see this other-side of Aylesbury. The hidden heart, as it were, which is both incredibly well hidden and incredibly beautiful. I could quite happily pass the rest of my days in one of the cottages opposite the church in what remains of the old quarter. Not that I am going to, mind.

The hidden nature of the past has turned me on to the hidden nature of the present and has thrown up the memory of a film I once saw in my youth and which has stayed with me ever since. For some reason it feels an opportune moment to discuss its content with Wen, who is currently engrossed in the draft copy of the book. But before I can launch into my opening gambit Wen pipes up...

...So Noin related to Aeth the advice she had received from Big-Boss Stud, and Aeth did as he was bid.

He went to Elkmar's house at Samhuin, and he went armed with the Sword of Light which Big-Boss Stud had given to Noin, even though it was a day of peace in Albion, when no man was at odds with his fellow...

..."From left to right as you look at it..."

"Say what?"

"The Twin Suns' window. It is the other way about in actuality. It is the window's right light which only looks left from your perspective." Wen is clearly in edit mode. What is perhaps even more infuriating though, is the fact that she is correct. "And vice-versa..."

And she knows Latin...

"Of course. An oversight, obviously. Thanks. Actually, it's funny that you should pick up on that..."

"Why's that then?"

"Because it reminds me of a science fiction film I once saw."

Wen puts down the draft, and smiles. "Oh really..." She is very indulgent.

"Yeah, the scientists on our Earth discover that there is another planetary body at exactly the same distance away from the Sun as the Earth only on the opposite side of the Sun and it is moving at exactly the same speed as the Earth too, so that it always remains behind the Sun from the perspective of the Earth."

Dragon of Earth,

61

Dragon of Heaven

"So how do they know it is there?"

"Well, that's just it you see because they don't for sure, so they decide to send a spacecraft with an astronaut in it to check out if this planet actually exists."

"And does it? In the film I mean."

"Well, we never really get to know for sure either actually."

"What! What kind of a crackpot film is this?"

"It's a genius film. They think something goes wrong with the mission and that the astronaut they sent up returns to Earth... never having reached his destination."

"They only think something goes wrong with the mission."

"That's right, and the astronaut that returns looks slightly different to the one they sent up."

"What do you mean, slightly different?"

"Well it's obviously the same bloke only his face is the wrong way around."

"What on earth are you talking about?"

"Well you know how our faces aren't quite symmetrical, say for arguments sake the left side is slightly smaller than the right..."

"As you look at it or as it is in actuality?"

"Yes, that. But forget that for the minute."

"Uhuh, but I've got you!"

"I know. Well, the astronaut that goes up, the left side of his face is smaller than the right, only the astronaut that comes down, the left side of his face is bigger than the right."

"He is about face... without being... about face. This is seriously freaky stuff."

"Isn't it? But it gets better. It takes a while for people to work out what's going on with the face thing and not all of them do, only I think the head of the mission does, and the astronaut's wife. Only, before they work that out the astronaut starts to realise things aren't right too."

"Like what?"

"Well, his house is the same and everything except that the light switches are on the wrong side of the door and everything is..."

"...opposite to where it should be! It's a mirror world and the other planet is a mirror planet, and they've sent out an astronaut at exactly the same time, only from the opposite direction, so the spaceships haven't collided and, oh my god, what happens?"

"Well, when they work out what has actually happened, no one believes them, so then they work out a way of proving what has happened..."

"..."

"...but that involves sending up another mission. I think it also involves a full frontal-facial photograph of the astronaut, which they cut in half and give one half to the astronaut..."

"Yes, I can see how that would work... I think..."

"Presumably, the other astronaut on the other Earth will at the same time be doing the same thing, only his half will be different so when they each get to their opposite Earths the photographs will be skew whiff."

"No... No... No! The photographs will be symmetrical. The photographs to start with would have been skew whiff."

That's what I like about Wen, she does not miss a trick.

"They might need to have photocopied the original photographs too."

"Undoubtedly. Anyway, as you can see, the plan, if it had worked would have proved the existence of the other Earth, only this time the mission does go wrong and the returning space-ship crashes killing the astronaut and destroying his half of the photograph..."

"Killing both astronauts and both halves of the photograph and along with them any hopes of proving the existence of the other Earth. Blimey! Is that the end of the film?"

"Not quite. The end of the film is the head of mission, who is wheel-chair bound, charging into a mirror at the end of a long corridor..."

"The mirror's a nice touch. Idea-wise, it does sound like a genius film but I have to say, even so, that what it actually describes is Twin Earths... and not Twin Suns."

"Spoil Sport..."

"And by the way..." Wen can be rather infuriating when she is in edit mode.

"Uh uh?"

"We may have to explain this 'our' business."

"Isn't it obvious?"

"Not if we're teaching non-attachment and non-identification it's not."

"'Our' is a term of endearment not ownership."

"Thank you."

"Spoilsport times two."

Elkmar was on the fair-mound, watching his youths at their games, and he had with him for protection only his white fork of hazel and the golden brooch holding his cloak.

Aeth approached Elkmar's person, drew the Sword of Light, and hewed at him with it, "You must grant me a request, O Elkmar, lest I

64

relieve you of your life breath."

Now, Aeth's request was that the lordship of the house on the river Avon be given over to him for the space of one whole night, and one whole day, and since Elkmar's life was dearer to him than his land, that request was indeed granted to Aeth.

...Wen is right. The film does describe twin Earths however in some respects what is seen from those two earths is a twin Sun. They are, at any one time, each party to a side of the Sun not accessible to the other at that time. From their point of view, although they do not know it originally but do eventually come to suspect it, there are two Suns in one. Bodies in space you may begin to realise are not quite as straight forward as at first they might seem. And this goes for our own bodies too. And our own minds for that matter.

There is absolutely no guarantee that I have remembered this film story correctly. If we struggle to see things that are staring us in the face in the present, how much more difficult to be accurate with the past and even with what we like to call our own past...

Wen, who is much more concerned with other people's pasts than I am points out a horse block in the courtyard which is now being used as a flower pot. A very effective and flower festooned flower pot it has to be said.

"Given that Anne Boleyn and King Henry the Eighth once stayed here during their illicit courtship, it is just conceivable that they could have used that horse block to mount their horses."

This it seems to me is a fitting note on which to curtail our repast...

...So Aeth had the lordship of the house on the river Avon for the space of one whole night, and one whole day.

And on that night it just so happened that he saw something, for the likeness of a young girl appeared to him, at the head of the bed where he slept: she was holding a bright, silver comb with gold ornamentation on it, and she was standing before a silver basin which had at each corner, four birds chased in gold, while around its rim went tiny gems of carbuncle; a purple cloak of curly fleece hung in folds about her, and was held fast by a golden brooch; her long, hooded-tunic was made of the smoothest green silk embroidered with red gold, and she had marvellous bow-pins of silver over her breasts; two tresses of yellow hair fell to her shoulders, and each tress was a weaving of four twists ending in a bauble of burnished red-gold which shone like the bloom of the iris in sunshine.

Aeth made to take the girl's hand and draw her to his bed but as he did so she vanished, and he woke up.

He remained in bed until the morning but he could not sleep because his mind was so vexed by the dream.

No food entered his mouth that day and when Elkmar returned in the evening to reclaim the lordship of his house, Aeth refused to give up possession of it.

At that a great dispute arose, and appeal was made to the judgement of Big-Boss Stud...

"I've just thought of another twin Sun!"

"Go on..."

"The Sun is responsible for the weather system *and* the water cycle."

"That sounds like heaven and earth again but..."

"But anyway, you know it's this notion of wholeness which is the real killer."

Wen and I are on the way back from our disappointment at Stowe and have called in at a village pub for a spot of luncheon. Coincidentally the pub turns out to have once been a coaching inn and also quite coincidentally it turns out to be a Queen's Head.

"How do you mean?"

"Well, if the human condition is anything at all, it is really the struggle to be whole."

"Not the struggle to survive?"

"Well, initially, yes... but then."

"And then the struggle to reproduce?"

"You're right of course, it can be something of a struggle can't it although I'm not sure it is strictly necessary."

"It is an imperative of the body."

"Undoubtedly, but that doesn't necessarily mean that it is... necessary."

"And yet wholeness is?"

"Absolutely necessary."

..."By right, the house and the land on the banks of the river Avon belong to the youth for all time," decreed Big-Boss Stud, "for he was granted the lordship for one whole night and one whole day, and what is it, if not in nights and days, that all of time, is made up?

"Even so," he said to Elkmar, "I will give you lands that are no worse than those you have lost, for the youth did hack at you, and threaten your life on a day of peace and rest. And you shall have from now until the Calends of May to make ready your new abode, for the Cleft House, and the three lands about it shall be yours, and the boys from that house to sport before you on each feast day, and the best of the fruit from the river Avon still for your enjoyment."

Elkmar was satisfied with that, so he set out for the Cleft House, and immediately began the construction of a fort about it, while Aeth wintered with Big-Boss Stud until the house on the bank of the river Avon became free, at which time he took up his abode there...

67

..."But isn't the desire to reproduce the same as a desire to be whole?"

"I think it is the same desire, but if it is then it is misguided, because reproduction can never be whole. It is always by definition divisive. You only have to consider cell division and the growth of the animal body to realise this."

"Aren't you confusing different modes of being there?"

"I am not confusing anything. There is only one mode of being. Wholeness. But anyone who seeks wholeness through reproduction is confusing the mode of being for a mode of non-being."

"One mode of being... A multitude of modes of non-being."

"One time... many times."

"Although, generically speaking, and also relatively, all lifetimes last the same amount of time. The life of a gnat although only one man-day seems to the gnat, at least, to last about seventy man-years. And for a cognitive Sun, seventy man-years would be one Sun-day."

"Three-Score years and Ten."

"Do we know why they divided into scores?"

"Not really. Twenty is almost three sevens?"

"Oh excellent. The science of 'nearlydom'!"

"A year and a day? A macro-cycle and its micro-cycle implies... eternity."

"I think it may even be cleverer than that."

"I'm all ears."

"A score is two tens anyway. So it's three periods of binary opposition or polarity resolved by a whole, as well as a macro-cycle and a micro-cycle."

"Is there anything instructive of that in the tradition I wonder?"

"There may be..."

Now, the sons of fifty lords came to serve Aeth and to make up the number of his household, and they were all of an equal age, and alike in form and appearance.

And Aeth's mother, Aini, gave him twelve of her own cows which were white, with red ears, and although he had no wed-woman his household prospered for eight years...

"...All of which, reminds me..."

Wen sighs. "Go on..."

"In the course of my recent studies, I have come upon a number of words which can be used to express a natural meaning and also... it's opposite." Although somewhat indulgent, even Wen gets a little weary sometimes, however, as one of my supervisors as well as my friend she is more or less bound to pay heed.

"How do you mean?"

"Well, take 'cleave' for example. Its primary meaning is to 'cling to' or 'hold fast' and yet it also means the complete opposite of that, 'to cut' or 'slice in two', 'to divide'."

"...lift up a stone..." says Wen.

"...I am there..." I say. "Cleave a piece of wood..."

"...I am there also," says Wen.

"There are others."

Wen smiles, she is clearly starting to enjoy this particular pub game. "How many others?"

"Well, I have come across another couple at least..."

"Which are?"

"Dash..."

"...To move quickly..."

"...and to be stopped in one's tracks." Wen smiles again.

"...and... execute."

"Execute?"

"To make, as in execute a good shot in tennis, and to un-make..."

"...as in to curtail a life." This is indeed a bizarre discovery although that particular example is perhaps a little strained.

69

I smile and say nothing as Wen notices for the first time the inn sign over my shoulder.

"You know, it looks almost as if the Queen's shoulders are hills and the Queen's head..."

"...is floating in the sky."

"Judging by the lower bar. It also looks as though the inn has changed its name."

"Or just the brewery..."

"Or just the brewery, although I have to say..."

"Here we go..."

"She doesn't look much like a Queen."

Head in the Clouds

...But at the start of Aeth's eighth year of residence he dreamt again of the girl whom he had seen on his first night, and now when she appeared to him she shook off her hood and loosened her hair in order to wash it in the basin, and so the cleavage of her breasts became visible to him through the opening in the halter of her tunic; snow the whiteness of a single night, was there over that wondrous plain; her neck was slender and straight; foxglove red her clear, lovely cheeks; her eyes, blue hyacinth; her eyebrows, beetle black; her lips, rowan berry red and her teeth a crescent of pearls. She was the fairest and most beautiful woman in the world...

❖

...Wen is still playing pub games. "Where would you put Dashwood then?"

Of course! Dashwood. I had not even considered Dashwood...

"Well at the outset he moves along quite merrily enough cutting his dash... before coming fairly seriously... unstuck."

"The baboon!"

"The devil's very own."

"His sun and star though, are nevertheless very interesting."

"His sun and star are nothing less than genius! Sixteen points of spatial direction... Does that preclude the star behind, being without?"

"I think it probably does. It is the same colour as the centre of the sun."

"Which also looks like it has an eye in it, although that could just be a flaw in the stone."

"Oh come on! He was rich enough to choose whatever stone he wanted and to change it if not satisfied."

"True, but in any case, get close enough... and a star is a sun..."

"Or at least, that's what we're told it will become."

"I don't know. Maybe it does just refer to process, or time, and the inevitable swing from one pole to another. There's a part of us that needs stable definitions."

"And a part of us that needs fluidity..."

"The letter... and the spirit... of the law..."

But when Aeth reached out to her in his sleep, to take hold of her hand, she disappeared as before, and he woke up.

He remained in bed until the morning but he could not sleep because his mind was so vexed by the dream.

No food entered his mouth that day and at night a vision of the same woman again came to him: she was plucking the strings of a tiompan with her delicate white fingers; long and tapering were her arms, her shoulders straight and smooth, and she walked with a steady, stately step; the light of the moon was in her noble face, the blushing dimples of courtship were in her cheeks, the gleam of pleasure in each of her two royal eyes, and a gentle, womanly dignity in her voice as she sang:

"O noble heron,
if wish you had
then one small fish
could make you glad;

yet I would wish the
sun down from the sky
but the sun it shines
and passes me by;

though leaves of gold
with silver fruit,
may hang from every tree;

so sad am I,
so sad... for my love
is far from me."

And that song so entranced and haunted Aeth that he could think of nothing else during all his waking hours.

72

...The Dead Letter and the Living Spirit of the Law...

"And never the twain shall meet."

"It is strange how words work, they're supposed to define things for us but the more you consider them, I mean *really* consider them, the more questions they throw up."

"Words work like worlds."

"And numbers work like worlds too."

"Worlds... and words... and numbers..."

"What is it that we struggle to express without the use of our clever yet ultimately clumsy symbols?"

...Half a year passed, and every night the same woman, in the same dream, singing the same song appeared to Aeth, so that he fell sick from the love of her, and no one could divine what it was that ailed him.

So Fern, the leech of Big-Boss Stud, was called. He could tell from a man's face what the illness was, just as he could tell from the smoke that came from a house, how many people were sick inside.

"No meeting this," said Fern when he saw Aeth, "but love in absence: you are grown sick at heart."

"It is true," said Aeth and he began to describe the beauty of the woman who appeared to him every night...

"No matter who she is," said Fern, "if love for this woman has seized you, then you must search the whole of Albion for her."

Now, the thought of finding that woman was enough to raise Aeth from his sick bed, and so he summoned the whole of his household and gave each of them instructions to search the expanse of that green land for her, and to bring him news when they had found her.

But though the sons of those fifty lords did scour the countryside both high and low for half a year, neither sight nor report, had any of them, of the wondrous woman which Aeth had seen...

"Of course, we all live in two worlds anyway... the waking world and the dreaming world."

"I'm not sure 'all' works actually... and 'live' is a bit dubious too."

"Well, we all have the potential to live in two worlds."

"Does the dreaming world have a Sun?"

"It has an interior Sun and all the characters which populate it are lit from within. That light though, is white light."

"So, it may just be that the interior Sun... is actually a Star!"

...So Fern summoned Big-Boss Stud to advise his son.

"I know of the woman whose beauty surpasses that of every other woman in Albion," said Big-Boss Stud.

"Then you must tell me where she is," said Aeth, "and I will journey there to woo her."

"She lives in the province of Lugdunum," said Big-Boss Stud. "She is called Very-White, and she is the daughter of Sweet-Mouthed Maeve and Aillil Silver-Tongue, but I would warn you, my son, a right dangerous and tricky couple are they to contend with."

"No matter, that," said Aeth, "for unless Very-White becomes mine, I shall surely die."

Chapter Five

FIELD OF SHEAVES

"However good... it could be better,
However bad... it could be worse..."
Endless Round

Wood-Stone

"However bad... it could be worse..."

But not much.

Wen insisted on coming over... and now... the whole scheme is shot to pieces...

Beyond the horizon, the dull orange glow echoes the crackling flames illuminating their faces. Shadows leap... dancing primal patterns across their skin... life and death woven in their stark brightness...

...It started well enough and our Lodge meeting was probably the best of the new era, with the re-introduction of a semblance of ritual and a very definite guided meditation. It looks like we are beginning to find our new feet. And perhaps we are, yet the bombshell of Wincobank Hill will take a long time to settle. A long, long time.

But wait, I was going to tell you about the wood-stone first. It sounds like something of an anomaly that does it not? Well it is not. It just means that the stone is in a wood now. Whether or not it has always been thus confined is highly debateable. I expect it has not...

...Eyes meet in silent communion.

There is resolve and determination written there, large as grief, much deeper than loss...

...As usual the authorities are all but clueless as to what it actually is or what it represents and that is largely due to their insistence on letting their minds do the looking. We touched on this when considering the

Atlantean Stone Cross and if you are wondering why I am insisting on calling it that when I know full well that it is nothing of the sort it is known as reverse psychology...

"Early fourteenth century you know..."

My Big Toe!

...He was tall, still.

She remembered when his hair was black as the raven's wing, when his voice was raised to call the stars down to weave the lays, when his hands were like ivory birds, fluttering between the worlds calling them forth into vision...

...But anyway, back to the wood-stone. The authorities are agreed on its antiquity. It is either Bronze age or Iron age if that can be termed an agreement which in 'sense-speak' translates as very old or really old. Either way, stones crafted in these 'ages' are not supposed to do or be what this stone is and does which, strange to say, makes me think that it is really very old indeed...

"What's all this about your big toe?"

"It's hurting."

"Do we know why?"

"We do."

"Would we like to elucidate?"

"My big toe is hurting because a rock from one of your beloved moors bit it!"

"You mean you stubbed your toe?"

"I may have done."

❖

...He is old now.

His hair is the colour of starlight.

His voice is deep as night.

His hands, as knotted as the staff upon which he leans.

She smiles... serene...

...But first to the finding, which was not easy and, which though I am utterly loth to admit it, was down to Wen.

I should have known then.

Turning up on my patch and finding things! Still I suppose Wen would say she is just getting her own back and in truth I am glad she found it because I was beginning to despair...

...She was small.

She had always been small, one of the ancient ones of the land.

He remembered the child she was when he had found her, the child of clarity in her heart as she had grown in knowledge and power, the child in her womb after the rite in the wood.

She was his child, his wife, his mother and sister, and his priestess...

She was all of these and more...

They were joined at the soul, children of the Gods.

The rowan berries in her hair shone bright against the faded honey.

Rowan; the tree of vision, mystery and power.

He would always see her now with berries in her hair...

...It does not help when you are following poor directions although, to be fair, we were also given precise co-ordinates and I do have a compass. It is just that when I considered going down that particular route it seemed, to my mind at least, something of a cop out, especially as Wen had also brought me some dowsing rods. The spare set which had finally turned up at hers. They were just like Wen's too with their own black velvet pouch and all. Neat!

Anyway I was fairly confident that the two of us would have more success than I had done alone. Especially as a bit of research revealed that we were in fact looking for a flat stone and not an upright as I had previously supposed. Looking with my mind the last time you see, and looking with the mind only works when you already know what the thing you are looking for looks like...

...He smiles, yes, he knows that for truth.
Always would not be long now...

It still took us longer than it should have though and that was in part down to the directions not specifying when to turn left and head into the trees looking for the clearing. Before or after the first stream (dry in summer). I mean, I ask you, "on coming to the first stream... turn..." It sounds like before does it not?

That is what we both thought and that is what I thought the last time I had looked and failed to find it and so that is what we both again did. It does not mean before though it means after.

And this from a so called scientist.

I know what happened. After giving the precise co-ordinates our scientist thought, "well nobody but a fool would deign to follow the directions after being given the precise co-ordinates"... and so he skimped on them.

79

Naughty, naughty Mr Science-Man.

Not only did he skimp on them though, he also made them fairly nonsensical. Listen to this, "after about seventy metres a clearing in the trees opens up and the stone is clearly visible. It may be covered, it may not..." Oh, Mr Science-Man! Covered with what? And since when has a covered stone, if it *is* covered, been clearly visible?

I do not mean to be critical, even though I am being, because Our Mr Science-Man, may the Lord God bless his soul, did get one thing right. The wood-stone is stunning.

Well, two things actually, because he also had the humility to admit that neither he nor any of his colleagues knew the purpose of the stone. And a third, for he was also possessed of the great good grace to enquire after any theories, of which, all in good time...

So all in all... not such a bad sort...

...Across the flames is a young woman little more than a child.

Behind her is a Guardian, one of those who served the sacred enclosure. Ever silent except to speak for the Gods.

Tall he stands against the distant glow, present, watchful.

A figure of fear and trust, he is the shield of the young one.

The almost-child weeps tears of molten gold in the fire glow.

Her eyes beg questions, plead for answers... yet they are silent.

The kinship of the three shines in their resolve.

It must be now.

There is no more time...

...But first the directions. Wen decided to ignore them completely and find the stone by way of Mr Pre-Science-Man which proved to be spectacularly successful. Only, she did not tell me that this was her plan and just sort of left me in the middle of the wood with the now very grubby looking directions in my hand and no stone in view.

One minute she was behind me conversing in 'direction-speak', the next she was not, and was instead, along with the stone, if it did indeed exist, nowhere to be seen...

❖

...The Clan of the Raven has withdrawn to the hills, to a high place in the sacred lands, nearer the centre. Their fires are dead, their hearths are cold and their hilltop is now silent under the moon.

Others come, others who are not known to the Gods, others who would abuse the knowledge and the power of this sacred place.

Their campfires burn beyond the far hill, a day's sight from here, they herald both an ending and a beginning.

Within the walls of this highest place, where the Raven-Folk have lived in peace, lie deep secrets.

Envy has brought the others.

They do not know as we know.

They are not ready to read the heart of the Land...

...She was gone a long time too. Long enough, for a prolonged search of the immediate area... and a prolonged retracing of our track... and a prolonged foray back to both the first and the second streams, all to have proven fruitless...

And long enough for me to have finally sat down on a tree stump by the path and started contemplating just how to explain the loss of one director of our school, to the other director of our school...

...The Clan withdrew, beyond sight.

The walls and palisade are stacked with oil-drenched wood.

The bowl shattered into a thousand shards.

The blade is broken.

The sacred flame extinguished.

Only the crackling blaze before them remains...

..."What do you mean you lost her?"

"One second she was there. The next she was not."

"Responsible people don't just go missing in the woods."

"This one did."

"Not when they are supposed to be with other responsible people."

"I know Ben... it's all my fault... I'm sorry..."

...The Lady of the Rowan Crown smiles loving encouragement and nods her head.

The girl-child, seeded with knowledge and Knowing gasps in smoky grief.

The Guardian passes her the flaming brand.

Blinded by tears, yet she smiles at those who stand beyond the flames, the two and the arc of those who remain with them, ghosts already in the twilit darkness.

She turns, supported by the Guardian and thrusts the brand into the tinder.

The flames crackle and leap into the night...

..."FOUND IT!"

"Where are you?"

"Over here!"

82

"Over where?"

"Here..."

"Wow!"

"Nowhere near where it's supposed to be, of course..."

...He leads her away, almost carrying her.

They disappear into the blackness beyond the ring of flames choking on the oily smoke, blind with tears.

Within the flames, a voice sings farewell to the stars...

..."So how did you find it?"

"I asked the fairies. I went back to the track, the proper track, found the portal trees, passed through them and it's more or less in a straight line but at a slight angle down from there."

More of the portal trees later.

So much for happy endings...

For the record then, we think that the wood-stone is a landscape model showing a hillfort and an adjoining ritual site. There is a processional way around the outskirts which leads into the site and also a river or possibly two streams running through it and a burial ground bottom right as we look at it...

These people were not supposed to be working in Three-Dee, but that is what we think it is and if you think about it, I mean really think about it, they must have been working in this way to achieve the incredible feats of engineering that they did. And there can be no doubt that these sites, all of them, without exception, are incredible feats of engineering...

"...Earth-works!"

"Earth works for you when you let it."

But where is it? That is what we do not yet know. Wen thinks it is close to the stone, and relates to the forest before it actually was a forest.

I am not so sure. Knowing the immense scale on which these people constructed their visions, it could even be Wincobank Hill, and that is where we are heading next...

The fires glow against the horizon behind them.
Far... far... away. She cannot see them with her eyes.
But she feels them still. She will always feel them.
Red... Like the Rowan...
Red... Like blood...

...Not that I really wanted to go...
But Wen insisted...

She had been brought to the wood. Half blind with tears and grief. She was dragged when she faltered.

She was carried when she failed, by the silent Guardian.

They had followed the stream while they could. They left no tracks... no broken branches... no trace of their passage.

Where the streams met he had doubled back, confusing any pursuit and the fire-glow had been there before her eyes... etching itself on memory with fingers of flame...

❖

...I have a bad feeling about this place.

But Wen insists and when Wen insists, not even graphic descriptions of the steepness of the hill itself could deflect her. So, here we are, half way up the climb, resting on a convenient wall and even from this point the view is impressive.

I have been up here before and while that is useful, because I can sort of remember where to go, it is also a part of what is worrying me so much. I have completely blanked the previous trip from my memory, although thin shards of it are now beginning to filter back into my mind, none of it is particularly encouraging. But then, it was a long time ago and maybe things have improved since then. Unfortunately, I am not terribly good at convincing myself...

...An owl hoots softly and she jumps...

The Guardian's hand is over her mouth...

It stills the cry that could not be allowed to escape...

His alertness absolute... His life is hers.

She is now the vessel of knowing.

But her survival and the survival of more than self is for now in his hands, a curious symbiosis.

They both serve...

When Wen insists...

Thankfully, the common ground opens up sooner than I was expecting and although I know this was not the way I previously entered the site, we will doubtless be able to find our way from here.

"This will do..."

Before we get too much farther into the common ground we come across a pleasant surprise in the form of a recently placed monument to the Brigantes.

It really is quite spectacular and cheers me up no end, reinforcing the notion that things may have improved up here.

That feeling though does not last long. One look at Wen when we approach the site proper and I begin to wish that I had been the one doing the insisting...

Star map of the Brigantes

They wait...

They are still and silent then until the flapping of wings in the branches tells them it is safe to move.

It is only an owl.

She sees the dark shape silhouetted against the stars for a moment as it glides above.

The dark wings seem oddly reassuring.

When Wen insists...

I leave her to her circumambulations and try to focus on what little good is to be seen about the place, which amounts to rowan trees, a whole raft of them.

They never fail to lift my spirits but here even they are struggling. They only serve to remind me that there is a rather sombre tale about a castle of rowan trees and under normal circumstances I would simply make a mental note to look it up when I get back home.

Yet, considering there also used to be a castle of sorts up here, it may quite possibly be the tale I really need right now. When I try to remember, it proves as recalcitrant as my initial sojourn up here. All I really get is that the Castle of Rowans was an illusion... a trap to lure the unsuspecting, into a slaughter...

On they walk, deeper into the woods.

They pass between a portal of trees and cross a small stream.

Then they plunge, deeper and deeper into the undergrowth until they reach a small clearing.

...And slaughter might very well explain it, looking at Wen's features... which I do not really want to right now because of the very obvious pain.

"They burned it themselves," she says kicking the vitrified rock and then continues her circuit. That is not good. Wen has already told me that she considers 'them' her people.

"Why did they do that then?" I try to sound inquisitive but I am not really and I do not really want to know. Not because I am not interested but because I know it is going to be just too awful.

"To protect their lore..."

"Written?" My voice sounds like hollow hills, echoing.

"No... They burned the Keepers, the practitioners... they were

87

too old to flee with the rest."

"The lore perished?"

"There was a young one... also a Keeper."

"This is *before* the Romans right?"

"Oh way... way... way before..."

"How did they generate so much heat?"

"Wood-lore... and oils... tree resins."

"They burned their own alive!"

"They used wood that gives off poisonous fumes. Yew... alder... holly. They did not burn."

"Even so..."

"Have you got the rods?"

Oh Lord...

The Way-Stone sits beneath the canopy, marking their route in its curves and lines. She has never seen this place but she knows the value of the carved rock.

Her people have been here.

The rock is clean... scraped of its moss. She knows its language.

She can read the white pebbles placed carefully in the hollow... three nights ago they were here...

And safe.

They have vanished into the heartland and the stones tell the way.

She sweeps away the pebbles. There will be no clue left for others to follow.

They will see the stone with eyes that cannot read.

...Well at least the rods prove unequivocal.

A couple of circuits from different directions and the rods point the same way. The spot is unmistakable and we sit, Wen and I, in the eye of the maelstrom, although it is now ostensibly quite calm. The way to describe it, I suppose, would be oppression. The place has an oppressive feel to it.

And that is all it is really, but it also has an insidious effect... on everything and I mean everything around it. There is a diseased tree growing close by which gives graphic illustration, with its black spots for green leaves, if that were needed.

Wen places her gifts and blessings. And I give a very brief... and ahem... somewhat sporadic resumé... of the death of Lug's father which is an infamous fratricide and one of the Tragic Tales of Albion. In some versions, at least, it does have a tremendously liberating resolution, if you can get there... and although I do struggle, perhaps understandably in the circumstances, I sort of manage it... in the end.

"Riders of the Shee
to me from every place still free..."

That is how Lug, the Lord of Light summoned the Otherworldly Hosts. He met his father Cian and his two brothers and together they set off for the four quarters of Albion. Cian went to the North, while his two brothers went East and West respectively and Lug, well naturally he went to the South...

"Riders of the Shee
to me from every place still free..."

It is not difficult to see how this might have been a ritual summoning, however Cian did not reach his quarter because on the very next plain he traversed he was spied by Brian and his two brothers and that was a bad thing.

A deep enmity existed between the Sons of Turan and the Father of Lug. Brian ran Cian through with a spear... and then he buried the body a man's height deep in the earth and covered it with rocks.

Thus was the first cairn constructed in Albion: the Cairn of Cian.

When Cian failed to show at the hosting, Lug went in search of him and found his father's body and divined who had put him there.

The recompense he demanded of the Sons of Turan was to raise three shouts of victory on the Hill of Midken, knowing full well that Giants lived there, a father and his three sons. Brian and his brothers managed to raise the three shouts, but died in the raising of them.

When they gained the Field of Fallen Warriors why, who did they find waiting for them but Cian. He welcomed them as the brothers they should have been and offered them a branch with three apples of wisdom growing on it. They each took an apple and bit into it...

"Peace up to heaven...
heaven down to earth."

...In a leather bag beside the tree they have left oatcakes and honey-wine. The Guardian feeds her, in spite of herself, in spite of grief and fatigue, she takes them.

The oatcakes are dry and she cannot swallow... her throat too tight with memory. He passes her the small flask of wine, strong, fiery. She drinks deep as the tears fall again.

Curling silently into the leaf litter, she sobs in silence until she sleeps...

She dreams of others in the wood, strange folk, not the invaders, but they are seeking the Way-Stone. She reads them... knows them... sees their hearts.

One who seeks and one who strays... The seeker wears the shade of the Raven.

He feels it but does not see its mantle around him.

He is the thinker: re-caller of the ages.

The other, the one who has wandered, she too walks winged.

She knows.

She watches.

Far-seer... Almost!

She raises her hands and asks the Way...

The dreamer answers, mind on mind, and a flicker of awareness passes across the other's face. The dreamer watches as the other walks to the portal and follows the unseen path to the glade and the Way-Stone...

She sends out a ringing cry in the sunlight....

...We know when we are through because we spot the way down the hill and as we set off down the track Wen starts to laugh.

"You've been sitting on a berry!"

The squashed berry turns out to be ink leakage from the pen I used to scrape away the moss from the stone in the wood. Gosh, the wood-stone? That seems like an age ago.

Why I put it in my back pocket rather than back in my shoulder bag is anyone's guess but one thing is for sure... the trousers are now all but useless.

"I never really liked them anyway," I concede whilst contemplating the viscous black mess which is now sticking up my fingers.

Wen finds this even more hilarious!

At least there is laughter on the hillside and a pair of relatively new trousers is, without doubt, a small price to pay considering some of the other sacrifices that have been made up here...

The fires glow against the horizon before them.

They are close now, very close. There is always a fire here, at the hearth-place of her people, the ancient Heartland.

Its gentle light beckons.

Trees block the horizon as they approach, weary, hungry... bereft. At the ford, a warning... a prisoner... one of them! He is staked beside the stream...

His hands bound and a noose about his neck, his throat cut. He is not of the Raven-Folk. They pass and she casts a blessing on the mouldering corpse. He too serves the Raven now.

For a moment it seems she hears joyful laughter and sees the strangers of her dream walk beside her, forging a path through the bracken.

Then her heart lifts... the Raven-Stone, sharp point of rock against the skyline, and the soft glow of the hearthfire beyond. The circle of stones her people call the Raven's Nest. She has never been here before, but she knows.

She is home.

Raven's Nest'

Chapter Six

SEVEN LEAGUE BOOTS

"Seeing green is being, seen...
Seeing blue is being, true..."
Endless Round

Castle to Tor

"I've been thinking... The Star which the Thelemites are concerned with is the Star of the Tarot...Major Arcana... Eighteen... The One and the Eight?"

"Do we need to concern ourselves with this?"

"We may do."

"There is also one large star in some depictions and seven smaller ones."

"The Star of Consciousness and the planetary bodies as veils of existence."

"The Dance of the Seven Veils..."

"The Crowley deck dispenses with the planetary bodies and just concentrates on the consciousness..."

"You mean he's claiming to have revealed the seven?"

"Or transcended them..."

"Could he have done?"

"Possibly..."

"I wouldn't put it past him."

"I wouldn't put anything past him."

Wen laughs. "If he were around now he could simply buy the first book...or write it."

...So Aeth went to see his mother, Aini, at the Cleft House.

He brought back fifty mantles for the adornment of his household: each mantle was the colour of a beetle's back with four grey corners and a brooch of red gold; fifty tunics of brilliant white with animal embroidery of gold he also brought back; with fifty gold hilted swords, and fifty silver shields with gold rims; fifty spears with fifty rivets of white gold in each spear shaft, and fifty coils of refined gold about them with butts of carbuncle and blades of precious stone which lit up the night like sun rays; fifty dapple-greys with for each, a bridle-bit of gold, a silver breast-plate with little gold bells, a crimson saddlecloth with silver threads, an animal-headed pin of gold and silver, and a horse-whip

94

of white gold with a gold hook at the end...

❖

..."Why fifty?"

"I'm damned if I know. It may be something to do with five as the number of man."

"They're not though particularly man-like this company, are they?"

"They're distinctly un-man-like."

"Fey?"

"Fifty could represent the negation of the five outer senses... five.. .zero..."

"The inner senses again?"

"Except technically, there is only one inner sense which operates in five different ways."

"There is, though, something artificial about it all, don't you think?"

"Something distinctly illusionary..."

"Or delusional..."

"You know that Aeth is Arthur?"

"Arthur was only half-Fey..."

"Is Aeth all-Fey?"

"He may be..."

"So, where is he going?"

"He is going to meet his destiny..."

❖

Then Aeth buckled around his waist the sword of light and set out for the Fort of Tower Hill at the head of his marvellous house-hold, and about him went seven hounds on silver chains with an apple of gold between each two hounds; before him went seven horn-blowers, with horns of gold and silver, their tunics many hued, their mantles shining, yellow their hair, three fools preceded each horn-blower, a diadem of gilded silver on their head, and over their arm a shield with an engraved spiral boss, and a polished strip of bronze inlaid along the sides; three harpers in right royal garb were about each fool, with harp-bags of kids-skin, white with dark grey eyes in the middle, their harps of red gold had the forms of snakes and birds and hounds traced in silver along their edge and as the strings of each harp were plucked these forms made circuits in the air about them...

..."Remind me again, why we are going to Cadbury?"

We are back in the Silver-Bullet and Wen is enjoying herself. She likes speed! Sometimes, when I ask her questions when she is driving she slows down. Sometimes she does not. Which, in the latter case, means that she is speeding whilst also talking to me at the same time. It is a sort of Russian-Roulette for Barge-Folk...

"Because I didn't get an opportunity the last time I was here."

"With Cathy? Why not?"

"Because Cathy, she just doesn't do hills."

"Oh yes, of course. Cathy doesn't do hills and Carly, she just doesn't do churches. Do you need to find yourself some new girlfriends perhaps?"

"Cathy doesn't do hills because she can't do hills. It is a physical impossibility for her and Carly is simply struggling to recognise the difference between the Church as a Body and the body of a church. She'll get through it."

"Forgive me. All this travelling in the heat can make something of an arse of one. It does though raise a practical consideration. How did the infirm get to these places?"

"The young were strapped to their parents. The aged were strapped to pallets or piggy-backed up depending on the nature and the level of their infirmity..."

"I must say, the Church as Body and the body of a church is a quite eloquent distinction, but isn't the Church also supposed to be the Bride of Christ?"

"Ahem?"

"So which one did he marry?"

"We may need a third distinction, the Church as Bride of Christ."

"And what about all the nuns. Aren't they supposed to be brides of Christ too?"

"You're right Don... you really can be an arse sometimes."

Part of my reluctance for these, what might be called, impromptu assignations are the inevitable ruptures they make in the overall scheme of things.

Once a pattern has started to form it is disconcerting to have to unravel it all, or even to amend it slightly, to accommodate the new strand, and even though I know that it is good for the flexibility of the mind, and really it is something that we should be doing all of the time, it is still an effort and as such is ripe for avoidance if at all possible.

Plus... it is another hill.

On a very hot day!

...The watchman at the house of Sweet-Mouthed Maeve and Aillil Silver-Tongue saw the fair company as they traversed the game-plain of Tower Hill. He ran to his lord.

"You have news from your lookout," said Aillil Silver-Tongue.

"I have O Lord," said the watch, "for there is a great host approaching the fort, and a nobler or handsomer company of men can never before have been seen in these lands; the wind that blows from them is such that my head may as well be in a vat of wine..."

...Still, as we make our way out of the car-park and look up there does not appear to be much of a hill left to climb. The Silver-Bullet, bless her aerodynamically modified sides, has already taken us up most of the height. There is, though, a plague of gnats playing along an extended stretch of the tree tunnel which leads up to the hill-top.

Wen and I both turn our back on them which allows us to see the advertisement for the nearby pub which has been strategically placed for those descending the height.

"Still looking for the castle?"

"At least that's lunch taken care of," says Wen and grins.

The thought of lunch and an invisible castle revives me. After all, what we have here is another Uffington. Looked at in those terms it is difficult to imagine anything I would rather be doing really, although I still somehow doubt that there will be anything as spectacular as Uffington at the end of this particular tunnel of trees.

Interesting how indolence passes from the body to the mind like that. The best way out of it is to move and to move quickly, so I put on something of a spurt to reach the top and leave Wen trailing.

"It's the thought of beer and food which does that."

...So the people of Maeve and Aillil went out from Tower Hill and the crush in order to see that marvellous company was such that sixteen of their number died from suffocation. Aeth and his host dismounted before the gates of the fort, they unbridled their horses and unleashed their hounds which hunted seven deer, seven foxes, seven hares and seven boars to the game-plain of Tower Hill where they were slain, then the hounds leapt into the river and caught seven otters and brought these to the Hill-Fort also...

...There is something otherworldly about walking up a hill, crossing that threshold between the heat of a summer sun and the cool

98

green of the trees. Glimpses of a landscape that conforms to what we have come to know as sacred are seen through breaks in the gnarled trunks, squirrels scamper busily along the branches and the inevitable sound of birds accompanies each breath.

Beside the track, steep banks rise, channelling our footsteps through a narrow passage, guarded by ancient sentinels, rooted in earth. As the trees thin and the shade gets left behind it is almost like pushing through a tangible veil as we emerge into the unprotected sunlight of the summit. Looking back, the tunnel of trees closes in verdant darkness behind us, shutting us off from the world we left some five hundred feet below.

A solitary figure stands upon the far bank... there are always three, it seems, somehow. Although I know he is only another walker... I see the glint of a spear and a cloak flapping in the non-existent breeze...

...Aillil sent a messenger to ascertain the business of the wondrous host and the identity of its leader.

"His name is Aeth, he is the son of Aini, and he has come from the river Avon with his whole household, out of love for Very-White," said the messenger when he returned.

Then Aillil Silver-Tongue and Sweet-Mouthed Maeve withdrew...

...Reality is now shimmering in the heat as the air sparkles and I remember that King Arthur sleeps beneath the hill of Camelot like a child in a giant's womb, ready to wake in the hour of need.

I plunge into the earth in search of a cool cavern, yet my feet stand on the sunlit grass as the Knight who is a Priest approaches.

I pull the furs about me against the chill, standing spear-straight in the winter sun.

He may not pass.

The Temple is mine...

Hers...

He may not pass without answer...

Behind me a crescent of acolytes await, with bowl and stone, oil and wine... I hold up my hand and he meets my eyes...

"Whither goest thou, Priest of the Sun?"

"I go hence into the Lowlands for the people are in need."

"What is that need?"

"The need is Love..."

"And what will you give for the passage?"

"I will give my heart's blood to the land."

He offers his left hand. A priestess steps to my side, holding the bowl and the razor sharp shard of blue flint. He is silent, save for a sharp intake of breath as the thick flesh at the base of his thumb yields to my blade. Blood, red as the holly crown I wear, wells into my bowl.

With blood and oil I mark him, the sign of passage paid.

I lift the cup to his lips... wine-steeped herbs that open the inner sight... bitter... part of the price...

He drinks, his eyes holding mine like a serpent. I like his strength. He is no fool, this one... he knows the true price of vision...

Passing the cup to the maiden, I take his hand and lead him into the dark womb of the temple...

"A multitude of the lords of Albion will besiege us if he takes the girl," said Aillil.

"It would be better to kill him now," said Maeve, "before he has a chance to bring down upon us a magical destruction."

"Pitiful that," said Aillil, "and a right dishonour."

"We will not be dishonoured," said Maeve, "for I will see to it..."

100

"...Remind me again why we are going to Cerne Abbas and not staying at Cadbury?"

Wen smiles and puts her foot down as if to teach me a much needed lesson. Not that it could go down much further, mind. To be honest, I am still in something resembling shock at the utter enormity of the place that is Cadbury. And that was just a side-show... the main event is yet to come.

It is a little disconcerting to constantly have your expectations so seriously outstripped by reality. I mean, okay, so we were gifted with perfect weather, but what was screamingly obvious about the place was its function which is still very much intact if the intimations I was getting up there are anything to go by. Wen could feel it too and possibly, well probably, even more intensely than me...

"Is it something only we can see I wonder?"

"And others like us."

"It must be, otherwise something would be done about it."

"It is, though, difficult to see what can be done about it..."

"It makes the artefact held at Winchester Castle look pretty pathetic."

Wen laughs. "It's amazing really. If you told them what it was they wouldn't believe you."

"And yet, some people are only too happy to fly across continents to marvel at a complete fake."

"Well let's be kind and allow them a symbol. It's really all they can understand."

"And then there is the romance of it all..."

"From ritual..."

"Of course... that was Ms. Weston too."

..."A welcome to this wondrous host then," said Aillil Silver-Tongue on their return to the messenger

"A right comely and splendid warrior, Aeth," said Sweet-

101

Mouthed Maeve.

"Bid them enter the keep," said Aillil...

...In the event, the drive from Cadbury to Cerne Abbas is just about long enough for the experience at the former site to have begun to wane... and when I say wane, what I am describing is the transfer from present-mind to memory-mind, something you inevitably find yourself contemplating more and more when on the road like this. And in any case we stop off at a passing church en route, which curiously enough has the seats within arranged in a circle.

"And what are the chances of that, after coming from where we have just been?"

"If there are twelve seats I am going to scream."

"My ears are safe then, there are thirteen."

"That's possibly even worse."

"You don't get to scream though."

It is a pleasant enough place with a couple of large, well-ornamented painted sepulchres which begin to make a lot more sense when painted, even though they are still way over the top, and there is also a miniature St James.

But to be honest, I am beginning to get a little impatient for the Big Fellow. The Cadbury experience has really whetted my appetite and well, quite possibly for the first time in a while, I feel like we are back on the trail...

"It was a good idea of mine to come down here after all, eh?"

"Donald Sams, wash your mouth out!"

"Don't tell me you're going to try and claim credit for this trip." Wen's foot goes down and the speedometer needle starts to rise rapidly...

A fourth of Tower Hill-Fort was then set aside for the company of Aeth and so they made a quick circuit of the house, from one entrance to the next; then they hung up their weapons, sat down and were made comfortable...

❖

...We must be mad...

The sun beats down from the early afternoon sky, in the high eighties. Don flops onto the grass beside the steep path eroded in the chalk... the white and green serving only to accentuate the now prawn-pink of his face. Mine, I fear, is just as bad. My shoes are white with the dust... not exactly sensible shoes for hill climbing, mere scraps of summer lace. Bees buzz in the wild orchids... strange beetles, black and blood red scuttle through the shade of the sparse grass... we really should have brought water...

...The harpers of Aeth played then, and twelve of Aillil's men died from weeping and sorrow.

"It is a Champion who has come," said Sweet-Mouthed Maeve and her lips curled into an inscrutable smile.

"Divide for us the food that has been brought to the house," said Aeth, and his carver, Lothur, strode to the centre of the house and divided the food for them. He divided each piece in his palm with his knife but neither skin nor flesh was touched and from the time that he became carver, no food in his hand was ever lost.

The food was distributed and the feast lasted for three nights and three days... and when it was over Aeth was summoned to the House of Congress...

...We should really have just taken photographs from the viewing point where you could actually see the giant, but then, it would have been wrong not climb it while we were here. Cerne Abbas isn't exactly on our doorstep. And it felt right to climb... to sacrifice our energies. There is something intensely physical about the place and that is quite apart from the thirty foot of erect phallus...

We continue to climb, gasping a stunted exchange on the surprise discovery that our giant possibly once held a severed head... no wonder we had to come here! The head, the club, the phallus and also a possible animal skin... all very visceral, immediate... brutal, almost...

By now we have graduated from prawn to lobster and the climb continues. Past the ritual enclosure of the Trendle, around the back and the hill just keeps on going... higher and higher, in search of the best view of the strangely familiar 'manger' of the landscape. Gorse in full bloom fills the air with perfume...

...“Will you give me your daughter?” said Aeth mac Aini.

“I will,” said Aillil Silver-Tongue, “so long as the bride-price is met.”

“Name it,” said Aeth.

So Aillil walked to the copper shuttered window of the House of Congress, unlatched the shutters and opened them. “Do you see the plain yonder?” he said to Aeth.

“I see it,” said Aeth.

“You must clear that plain of stones, uproot and burn the thickets of thorn, then plough and sow the ground with linseed,” said Aillil. “When the seeds have grown, the stems must be culled and their fibres teased and spun, into linen,” he went on, “in order that a fine and fitting head-dress for Very-white, on the night of her wed-fest, might be woven.” But then he added, “And all of this must be done, within the space of one whole night, and one whole day.”

“It shall be done in that space,” said Aeth, and he went out from the House of Congress...

❖

...We stop, looking out across the processional way... Torchlight approaches. The sky is clear and the Hunter's Moon illuminates the white outline of the giant.

From the Trendle comes the sound of drums beating... soft and insistent, an echoed heart-beat of earth. The truncated scream of the stag pierces the night as the drum-beats increase their rhythm, pounding like blood through the temples, then dying down to a soft thrumming which waits...

She watches from the hill-top. There will be blood tomorrow too... for vengeance, for betrayal... for a kingdom. Many will fight for her... many will die... but she holds the power.

They will come, over the hilltop, through the valley... and they will be caught. She has the high ground and those who serve her know its ways...

But tonight she watches and waits. There is another service... she watches the dark forms approach from the enclosure. The man is bound with the skin of the stag, but not immobile... naked and washed with pure water from the spring, oiled and perfumed, beautiful in his youth...

She holds her blade before her... speaking to he who is led... drawing the sharp point, almost gently, across his skin. Marked with the blood in spirals... tracing them with the blade and watching his body respond...

"Whither goest thou, Priest of the Sun?"

"I go hence to the hillside for the land is in need."

"What is that need?"

"The need is Life."

"And what will you give for the passage?"

"I will give life."

She draws the maiden to her side. She too is naked and blooded, but unbound. Her hair falls in a long cascade, glinting in the moonlight. She places the maiden's hand on his and nods... the two are led away onto the hillside...

The drums begin again, softly at first, but with growing insistence, thrumming in the blood... rising, louder, faster... mirroring the rite on the hillside, reaching fever pitch... Life and death... this hillside will see them both... generation and destruction...

She watches...

Now, as evening drew in, the warriors of Aeth's company gathered themselves together, and at a sign from him, they did repeatedly hurl down their bright spears, and so pulverised the stones which lay on the game-plain of Tower Hill, while Aeth's fools, with their bright shields did, one by one, uproot the thickets of thorn which grew there, even as Aeth himself went amongst those thickets reducing them all to ash.

Then did Aeth summon from the western hills, two long-horned oxen, the one was yellow, speckled white, the other was white, speckled yellow, and yoked together they did plough the game-plain of Tower Hill in but an inkling of time.

And then did Aeth's company sow linseed in that game-plain throughout the night, so that a full nine hectares where sown, and as the sun did rise, so the harpers of Aeth's company did play the linseed up from the earth, and into the light, and they kept on with that music until the flax, along with the sun, had reached its height, when with a blast the horn-blowers blew, and those lofty stems did fall.

Then was the woody fibre of the stalks plucked, and teased, and spun by the nimble fingers of Aeth's harpers, and finally woven into a gossamer-like, sun-kissed head-dress, just as evening came down over Tower Hill.

Then Aeth picked up the head-dress, took it to the House of Congress and presented it to Aillil Silver-Tongue and Sweet-Mouthed Maeve. "Your bride-price met," he said, "your daughter into my keeping."

"A right clever and resourceful fellow you," said Sweet-Mouthed Maeve, "but before we allow our daughter into your keeping, I would

106

that you could find for me honey that is nine times sweeter than the honey of a virgin swarm, without drones and without bees, and bring that honey here before me, that I might taste myself of its sweetness."

"That honey shall be found," said Aeth and out he went from the House of Congress...

...It is yet another curious thing.

The first time I became aware of Maiden Castle I was in the Castle of Maidens. Of course at that time I did not know that what I had seen was Maiden Castle and anyway, I was also doing my best to ignore it.

"*Seen* seen or seen in vision?"

"Seen seen. Lee, Kerry, and I were in Edinburgh for the third of our ritual magic workshops. In fact I think we'd finished, only we'd arranged an extra day there to check out some of the bookshops and we had just made a few purchases in said bookshops and were on our way to grab some lunch. We were taking a short cut through the Grass-Market and there was an exhibition there, you know the type of thing... a series of metal-framed pictures set at an angle in a public space... can be quite effective I suppose, given the time..."

"Only you weren't giving it time."

"I know, and that too is curious. I mean I'd clocked it and that is what had pulled me out of our way, which was I suppose a sort of 'bookshop-short-cut-lunch' type way..."

"..!"

"But because I'd headed off, Lee and Kerry followed, so I sort of diverted and looked at the next scene along instead, which was of absolutely no interest what-so-ever actually."

"What was it?"

"Oh, some docks or other."

"What was the theme?" laughs Wen.

"Large man-made structures I think. Anyway I left Lee and

Kerry looking at the docklands and probably thinking, "Don has some very strange interests," whilst all the time I was casting over my shoulder and appraising the scene previous."

"So why did you do that?"

"I don't really know. I think I sort of thought that it wasn't in this country. That it was just too huge a thing to be in this country and for me not to have actually heard of it."

"...?"

"Plus, I'd just bought a couple of books, the implications of which were still whizzing around in my head and I didn't want to set off on another major mind adventure, especially as lunch was imminent."

"Ah... lunch was imminent. You're just a slave to the body."

"Aren't we all? Terrible really. I am constantly amazed at how dense I can be."

"You still got there though."

"Eventually, but more by accident than design."

"There's no such thing!"

"As accidents?"

"As design!"

...The next morning, Aeth went to the river and there he came across Very-White, resting by its waters. She was wearing a robe of flame-red silk about her, and around her neck went a torque of red gold studded with pearls and rubies. No gaze was there fairer than hers.

"O Very-White, long have I dreamt of this moment," said Aeth.

"Welcome Aeth," said Very-White, and her voice was like harp strings, plucked from afar. "Long too, have I awaited our meeting."

"Will there be a time for me to sleep with you?" said Aeth.

"Though the lords and nobles of Albion have sought to bed me since I was but a girl, none have obtained me for I have loved only you from that time on," said Very-White. "It is no false love that has brought you to me, Aeth, I will be yours alone for as long as you may desire."

Then Aeth approached Very-White, and kissed her lightly on the lips...

❖

...The hawk greeted us as we began the ascent to Maiden Castle.

We had seen the aerial shots but thought it looked a little nondescript from the road. We were wrong. The place is vast. Approached through a maze of ramparts and ditches that are so high and so deep they seem wrought by giants, well, they would... The effect is immediate... utter disbelief at the scale of this thing... astonishment... and a deep peace...

We are not the only ones to feel it and we pass with silent respect two youngsters in deep and heartfelt meditation on the Eastern rampart.

It is early, but we are, it seems, in a Temple of the Sun as the golden rays flood the land with light and warmth. We walk, following the footsteps of ravens that lead the way. Following the contour of the hilltop... it would not have felt right to do it any other way.

Halfway along the southern edge, we pass a depression in the ground, full of thistles and clouds of butterflies, symbols of the soul. What it was supposed to be we do not know. What it now appears to be is a vortex of swirling, pulsing, shifting energy that morphs and changes as we watch, disorienting and strange.

It appears to mark a change in the plateau. The land rises slightly... there is a division... the lower plateau is secular, the higher is not. I feel this was where the priesthood lived and worked and were trained.

We walk on, reaching the Western gate and there we sit. We talk for a while but there is something in the place that invites silence. I sit, cross-legged, in the centre of the gates facing out across the plain to the hills beyond. From here I can see the labyrinth beneath me. It feels right, somehow... my place... as if I could sit here all day. Time has no meaning here. Don lies back flat on his back and closes his eyes. He opens them again and directly above him a red kite soars... we look at each other and then back up at the bird... we have seen no kites since we left Buckinghamshire...

Somehow, we know we have to move. We walk out from the gate into the labyrinth. Was it defensive? Perhaps, but I feel this was not its primary purpose. It is a simple design, yet I, who am never lost, feel so now. I cannot get a grip on where I am and the strangeness gets to me. Turning a corner I see a man... or not a man... very tall, dressed in unfamiliar garb, masked and armed. I see him as clear as day. He stops me in my tracks... then I blink and he is gone.

Don has wandered off ahead and does not see, but I am in shock. I hurry after him, tell him of the Guardian. I now know what happened here...

...So Aeth returned to the House of Congress.

"That honey which is nine times sweeter than the honey of a virgin swarm, without drones and without bees," said Aeth, "if, it is that you wish before you, to taste of its sweetness then listen now."

For just then Very-White was walking past the House of Congress. She was playing on her tiompan, and her sweet voice rang out;

"O love that none might name,
by love's strange ways you came
that love may light our hearts in flame;

love's flame it burns,
as only love's flame can;

it burns two hearts
when two hearts
flame as one."...

..."Whither goest thou, Priest of the Sun?"

"I go hence to the High Place for the soul is in need."

"What is that need?"

"The need is Light."

"And what will you give for the passage?"

"I will give my Self."

He is naked save only for a white cloth around his lions... he has left all else behind as he embarks on this journey. She looks deeply into his eyes, reading his soul's truth there. This is the final test. If he fails he will not survive.

Many years she has watched as they have come and gone, many she has seen and taught, many have failed, some have succeeded... only those with hearts that see true. The labyrinth is woven, energies crackling and shifting between the ramparts, almost visible in the moon-dark night. Line and spiral, blade and vortex... all wait. She leads him between the two fires that mark both the entrance and exit to the labyrinth... though which one is which only few will ever know.

She marks his brow with a kiss and raises her hands...

At her signal, the fires are extinguished with a hiss of steam and a cloud of smoke. The plateau is dark... there will be no flame to guide him. It is silent. There will be no sound to draw him back.

He is naked and bereft as a soul new born. In limbo now, awaiting a birth... or a death...

The gates close behind him and she ascends to her place on the edge, facing the morning that is so far away. Her place... where she will watch...

..."A right cunning and resourceful fellow you," said Aillil Silver-Tongue. "It is with good grace and great gladness that I allow my daughter into your keeping. The preparations for your wed-fest shall be undertaken," and then he smiled, "but there is one thing more that we would ask of you before the arrival of that happy day."

111

"Then ask it," said Aeth.

"There is a Rowan tree that grows on an isle in the river," said Sweet-Mouthed Maeve, "its berries are of the brightest hue, and if only they could be gathered, they would surely go to make a brew of the headiest mead for the wed-fest of our daughter, yet because of the swirling current of the river which flows about that isle, no one has ever been able to pick its sweet fruit."

"I will pick that fruit," said Aeth, as he again went out from the House of Congress...

...Her eyes adjust to the heavy darkness and the change comes, shifting her vision to that other sight. Below, he too waits, that his eyes may adjust to the night and his feet walk true. He begins, walking carefully, treading the labyrinth with purpose and intent. He walks the first straight beneath her, he feels her there and looks up, futile though it is in the dark with the blackness of her robe pulled around her like a cloud. She smiles... he knows... she has hopes for this one...

West he turns, her eyes cannot see him but she walks each step with him.. Another straight, another bend... and a sword at his throat. The Guardian towers over him and he freezes... had he been walking faster the sword would have pierced his throat. The Guardian speaks a ritual question. He has been given no answer... he has to Know...

The voice whispers into the night and the sword is lifted

He walks on. Through the rough grass and stones, barefoot. Another Guardian... a spear at his chest... no words this time... only a gesture. He responds and the spear is withdrawn. Again a corner, a straight... the meandering path like the fleeting thoughts of the mind turns every which way...

A blade at his belly... choices to make in silence, only the Knowing to guide him. And another, and yet another... She walks with him, feeling every step from her perch...

Only the last now.

He is pushed to his knees, a sword across the back of his neck... a cauldron before him. A whispered response and a flame is given.

Below her the light of a single torch illuminates a small, flickering patch of the hilltop. On the horizon the first blush of dawn. It has been a long night...

A knock on the gates, firm and confident. They open... she stands between. The sun gilds the morning as she embraces him.

"Whither goest thou, Priest of the Sun?"

...So Aeth went down to the river, to where the current flowed swiftest, and Aillil Silver-Tongue and Sweet-Mouthed Maeve, along with their daughter Very-White, and all the hosts of their people went with him.

He unbuckled his Sword of Light, took off his clothes, and dived into the water.

"Do not come out," cried Sweet-Mouthed Maeve, "until you have gathered nine branches of the Rowan."

So Aeth laboured against the swirling river, reached the isle and gathered nine branches from the tree, which he quickly bundled together, and strapped over his shoulders. Then he set off once more swimming back through the broiling water to the riverbank.

Very-White said afterwards that whatever beautiful thing she saw, she thought it more beautiful to look at Aeth across the dark water, his body white, his hair yellow, his shapely face, broad above and narrow below, his eyes blue, with nine branches of the Rowan hanging out over his head, their red berries between his throat and his white face, such that she never again saw anything to match but a third of his beauty.

As Aeth brought the branches from the water Aillil Silver-Tongue cast a five pointed spear at him, it went through Aeth's chest and out through his back...

...They do have something of the 'otherworld' about them these places. Not so much Giant Hill itself perhaps although it may have been different had we gone into the Trendle. It fact I am pretty damn sure it would have been different in the Trendle. Wen was all for it... even with the helicopter buzzing us overhead. And her logic was very persuasive.

"No unauthorised person beyond this point," said the sign.

"But we are more authorised than anyone ever could be," said Wen.

It is difficult to disagree but then the village of Cerne Abbas is in itself quite otherworldly too. I got exactly the same feel from it as when I first went to Glastonbury. It felt like we had left England and gone abroad, perhaps to France.

"Albion!" smiles Wen. "The whole of these Blessed Isles used to feel like this..."

...Then was a strange thing heard; it was the sound of weeping over Tower Hill.

"It is the lament of my mother and her women," said Aeth.

Then three times fifty women were seen on the riverbank who were all alike in age, and form, and beauty; equally fair, comely and graceful, so that there was no way to tell them apart. They had the aura of the otherworld about them and they were dressed in purple silk with green head-dresses, and silver bracelets on their wrists and as Aillil's people crowded around that wondrous host, they became faint on the perfume emanating from them. A company of horn players went before the women, and as they played, their music was such that thirty of Aillil's people collapsed to the ground in rapture at the sound of it.

"Take me away," said Aeth to the crafty folk as they uttered their lament, and he was lifted and carried by the women into the fair-mound of Tower Hill...

...And then we come across the church. Cue mass excitement as we take in all the giants, which appear to sprout from every orifice. The body of the church you see is an education in itself. You probably already know about consecrated ground and unconsecrated ground. It is the Inner and the Outer, pure and simple. And this symbolism is carried into the structure of the building.

The gargoyles, the Sheelagh-na-gigs, the green men, the giants, the dragons and the like, they are all on the outside of the church building. They do not make it into the 'ark'. The inside is for all the saints and angels. Do you see? It is the same symbolism.

The Inner and the Outer.

Only this symbolism is in some churches carried even further...

"You mean it is three-fold. It is a three-fold symbolism..."

"Yes, my dearest Wen, the body of the church employs a three-fold symbolism."

"So what is the third fold?"

"In some churches the altar which has always been conceived as feminine, the Shekinah, because it holds things, is hollow and within the altar is placed... a stone phallus."

...Then Very-White turned to Aillil Silver-Tongue and Sweet-Mouthed Maeve and cried out:

> "A curse be on you both for this deed,
> a black curse, on you, in your pride,
> to put the death dues on your kin,
> by the fervent water's side;
>
> my faith and pledge, I'll keep
> with Aeth; he is my only love,
> though the river sands be under

115

his head, and the still waters above;

red fruit, the stain of my lover's
blood, red fruit stain red my breath,
let all fair hearts that long for me,
be emptied by love's cruel death."

"Wen..."
"Now."
"I know now."
"What do you now know?"
"I know why the hillforts feel so different."
"Why do the hillforts feel so different?"
"Because they're built inside the Earth."
"So how come we can see them?"
"Because once built... they're then turned... inside out."

Chapter Seven
MAN-HERD

"...the Beams of the Sun drive away the Night.
They destroy the stolen power of the Dissembler..."
The Magic Flute.

...and not just the beams of the sun...

117

In the Land-of-the-Living-Heart:
Brig and Weland Mind-Weld are playing fidchell...

Brig: Wen to Blakey-Topping.
Weland Mind-Weld: She'll never get there.
Brig: But I have a poem for her.
Weland Mind-Weld: Which she'll never receive.
A Mist on Blakey Topping...
A Mist of Mists on the Old-Wives Way...

One of the major disappointments about the aborted Scotland trip was missing Pickering. The original idea was that it would be the finale to the first book. That was way back in the day when we still laboured under the delusion that we had any say in the writing of these books. When we drew up elaborate chapter plans and plotted story arcs. When we headed out with a definite itinerary that Wen had spent days putting together only to have it, and all our story plans, well and truly shredded and usually before lunchtime.

Ah... yes... Many the times and oft' have I sat in some weather-beaten wayside pub drowning my sorrows over yet another lost plotline.

"That's also known as any excuse!"

Not anymore.

These days we have a rough idea of where we ought to be going and then just head out in that general direction and see what happens. Something usually does, even if we end up getting utterly lost and find nothing, at least we get to laugh about it later, as well as the opportunity to analyse what we should have done and where we went wrong. It is usually pretty obvious when you look back.

The 'Roman road' was a case in point, although in our defence the putter-up-of-signs was also doing his utmost to keep us away from it. The thing is that we have become accustomed to having the luxury of revisiting places when we miss things, or do not quite get the right shot, or our research suggests we need to go back. And that is fine when we are working on our own doorsteps, but when we are further afield the chances are it will be a while before we again get such an opportunity.

We are only just beginning to realise that on this trip and I have in mind a particular church we noticed on the way out to the Bride-Stones which we passed up thinking we could catch it on the way back, only to go back a different way. An obvious error to make. Neither of us can remember what it was called or where it was although we do have a rough idea of its vicinity...

Anyway, we made Pickering a primary focus of this trip, staying quite close in Cropton and we were not disappointed. Although much later than most of our other painted churches, the walls at Pickering are quite simply sublime. All the usual scenes are there, many of which we have only before seen in fragmentary form and there are also a few new ones. The depictions of St Catherine's martyrdom are particularly moving, perhaps because these atrocities are perpetrated on a woman.

And there is also a full-blown St Edmund, the original patron saint of England, who I initially mistook for Sebastian, because they are both usually shown with a body pierced by arrows... thirteen in this instance.

What is it, I wonder, about stories told in pictures that appear to be so liberating? Is it merely the aspect of personal interpretation alone that is so appealing, or something much deeper?

Needless to say, our primary interest was the dance of Salome and the beheading of St John the Baptist and it is well and truly present in all its graphic glory. The pseudo-page who wields the sword is, in his apparel at least, suggestive of our friend the Jester from Chalfont St Giles and the angel at Broughton St Lawrence, so we can be sure that we are not just dealing with the quirks of a particular artist or two. Interestingly enough, the story needs to be read from right to left as we look at it, otherwise it makes no sense whatsoever.

Then there is the depiction of Christ's Harrowing of Hell. First out of the Maw is Adam carrying the apple, now whole again, which he hands to Christ, behind him is Eve and all the fallen now divested of their genitalia. And that is not something you see every day of the week, or on any day of the week for that matter. I suppose I am thinking Sun Day. It is becoming apparent that the Christianity experienced by mediaeval man, peasant or otherwise is not the Christianity we experience today. Obvious really but for the discrepancies to be so gulf like, that is a surprise.

The other impressive thing about Pickering church is that it has a collection of books for sale on subjects of related interest. Fifty-odd churches in and at last we find one with a bit of nous... in Yorkshire!

It feels like some sort of reward for our dedication. As an indication of just how impressive the painted walls are in this church we are in there a good hour and I do not even look at any of the stained glass windows. We would have been there longer too only the vicar arrived to prepare his service...

THE HOUSE THAT FISH BUILT

Howden Hill

King Grim-Gaze, the slug-man, planned a great feast at Red-Hill-Hall. Said Grey-Sway to Father Fish, "Wake up, wake up! You must undertake a work of construction: a mead house for my father's banquet is required; it is to be completed a year from this day."

So, Father Fish set about his work, and one morning Little Nipper came to him and said, "Soon you will finish your labour, you must not seek payment until the cattle of Albion are brought before you, when this is done you must choose from among them all the white, black-maned cow."

Father Fish did as bidden by Little Nipper and, with all the cattle of Albion before him, he asked only one white, black-maned cow as the price of his labour. Now that seemed right foolish to King Grim-Gaze but he consented all the same...

"What's going on with the cow then?"

"It's a sacrifice."

"How is it a sacrifice?"

"Instead of asking for material payment. A symbolic payment is requested."

"I'm still not quite sure I get it."

"The symbolic is higher than the material. So the sacrifice of the material benefits that could have been gained guarantees the success of the venture in a higher sphere."

"And the Slug-King, Grim-Gaze doesn't get it either?"

"He's hardly likely to... as a Fomor, he doesn't even recognise the symbolic let alone its potential power in sacrifice."

"Remind me again what the cow is symbolic of?"

"The cow symbolises the moon... and dispensation... and in this case it also symbolises polarity..."

"Because it's black and white!"

121

...Back outside Pickering church, the working day is winding to its close so we take a pew on a bench in the village square and watch the world wind down. While we are watching the world wind down, three ravens are watching us from a roof-top over-head. When they are quite sure we have clocked them they fly off the roof-top together and back over the church...

"What's back up that way?" asks Wen.

"Let's go see..."

A short walk reveals Pickering Castle with high on its castellations three ravens cackling and preening.
The castle is about to close but when we look left we see a familiar looking hillock just over the way. The ravens fly up off the castle walls together and over to the hillock.

"It can't be can it?"

"It could be..."

"It isn't marked on any of the maps."

"Well... it looks like a hillfort..."

"And it wouldn't do any harm to have a look..."

"If we can find it..."

"And if there's a way to the top..."

We do find the hillfort, if such indeed it is, but it is barb-wire fenced around the base for sheep grazing. We do, though, manage to get what we think at the time are some good shots of the terracing.

"Can you take a close up of one of the sheep?"

"Why?"

"Well I'm thinking of calling one of the chapters, "Legends and Lies.""

"And?"

"Well you know how a lot of stuff is, shall we say, misleadingly labelled?"

"What in museums and art galleries and the like?"

"Amongst other places. Well, we could very obviously mislabel all the pictures in that particular chapter to make the point... just an idea."

"So the sheep would be?"

"A llama..."

Wen laughs... and a moment or two later thrusts the view finder in my face... "Lammas the Llama."

"Ba...aaaaa."

The house that Father Fish built was constructed in this way: it had nine compartments from fire place to wall, with each facade made of bronze, standing thirty feet high; it took a wagon team to haul each beam, and the strength of seven men to fix each pole.

At the front of the house, high above the rest, a royal compartment for King Grim-Gaze was erected, and positioned around it in a circular fashion were twelve couches replete with blankets and cushions for the comfort of the heroes of Albion.

In the roof of the house Father Fish constructed a sun bower with a cunningly crafted spy-hole so that he could look out over the feasting without being seen.

"I spy?"

"I see I... with an eyrie eye... Know what I mean? Know what I mean? No eye..."

"Or know I."

"You know some of the gospel accounts cannot be eye witness?"

"Why?"

"Because there is only the Christ and one other and the other is not an evangelist."

"You're thinking of the temptation."

"I am thinking of the temptation."

"Well, Mark gets it about right, he writes, "...and immediately the Spirit driveth him into the Wilderness... and he was there in the wilderness forty days tempted of Satan and was with wild beasts; and the angels ministered to him." And that's probably as much as one can say... if the tale has been reported, yet both Luke and Matthew go into massive amounts of detail."

"They do but that detail may be a part of the rite."

"A part of which rite?"

"The rite of Baptism which it immediately follows but which if we read from right to left instead of from left to right it actually precedes."

"And the Satan is?"

"The Satan is... the initiating Priest."

"And you accuse *me* of trying to get us hanged!"

"The 'Satan', as in the Book of Job, the prosecutor of God: the opposition. It makes more sense to be tested before the descent of the Spirit than after it."

"You know you might be right."

"I am right. If I were to ask you who Jesus would be likely to meet if he were to head out into the wilderness what would you answer?"

"..."

"Whose voice is it that cries *in the wilderness?*"

"John the Baptist's."

"How does he prepare the way for the Lord and make his path straight?"

"By testing him."

"Hey! What happened to our sun?"

Wen and I are back in the Silver-Bullet and heading out to Blakey Topping. I had not realised the link between the Hole of Horcum and Blakey Topping the previous day and that is probably why we went so badly astray although the 'Roman road' we were looking for is not necessarily Roman and is also known as Wade's Way, and Wade is another giant... as is reputedly the fellow responsible for hollowing out Horcum Hole and depositing the debris right about where Blakey

Topping now stands. The more prosaic explanation inevitably involves ice flow, although it is just possible to resolve the two accounts by realising that what the Norse described as frost giants, *were* ice flows...

"I don't know, but this definitely wasn't forecast."

This turn in the worst for the weather is bringing back memories of yesterday's debacle and already making me feel somewhat uneasy about the whole Blakey Topping thing.

"It is beginning to feel like someone or something does not want us to get there..."

"Don't be daft. Who could possibly want to prevent us climbing a hill? You'll just have to look upon it as a test... It is though incredibly spooky."

"Incredibly spooky." A Range Rover full of people passes us, slowly, edging tentatively through the mist which swallows it whole in a matter of seconds.

"Remind me again. What is it we're looking for?"

"A big hill!"

"Which is unmissable right?"

"Even in this mist it is unmissable."

"They do wander about though."

"What wander about?"

"Sacred hills... I'm assuming it's sacred."

"It looked sacred on the photograph... what do you mean they wander about?"

"Well, they sort of disappear and stuff..."

"...They disappear and stuff?"

"Yeah, they're sort of not where you expect them to be and then you turn a corner not expecting them and there they are, looming up at you bigger than they ought to be...'

"Yeah, Barrow Mump did that, if you remember?"

"I remember. I mean how precisely do hills of such size do that? How does a hill that size, manage to play hide and seek... and win? Anu, our human-eyed, game playing dog-friend would be proud."

"Glastonbury Tor does it all the time. You can't even see it from the town."

"Maybe that's what makes them sacred in the first place. That initial sighting and the feeling it inspires which inevitably produces utterance. We've had seeing hills maybe these are hills of utterance."

"Maybe you're right. There's a very obvious linguistic link between word and lord in English. And although it was probably accentuated in the Bullet-Car, even if you were walking and always presuming that was an ancient track we were on, you'd turn the corner and... oh Lord! And that's how you know it's a sacred hill of utterance..."

"That happened with Howden Hill too..."

"It did... Oh my word! It's there, that's it..."

"Woo-hoo..."

"Oh, my Lord! It's huge... look at it!"

"...My word!"

It looked as though an invisible giant had slowly stooped, delicately picked up the edges of the mist and with a flourish and a twisted grin had lifted it... just as we had turned the corner of the descending spiral of the hill-track, straight in line with Blakey Topping... like some vastly oversized magician revealing a rabbit, or better, a dove.

"It's a sacred hill alright."

"A sacred hill of utterance..."

"Not a 'Woo-hoo' hill then?"

...King Grim-Gaze issued a proclamation: "Unless the men and women of Albion partake of my feast, I will stir up strife between father and son until mutual slaughter results, and I will set mother and daughter at blows until their breasts become loathsome and putrid."

...When we finally calm down, after quite some considerable time, we start trying to assess whether or not our new-found 'Sacred

Hill of Utterance' is approachable.

The road we are on leads through a farm, so we are guessing that it is private property. There is, though, both a bridle track and a footpath at an angle to the road.

The bridle track, which presumably leads to the Bride-Stones and the foot path which may lead to a way up to the crest of Blakey Topping, although from this vantage it is not possible to say for sure, because while the mist has gone from the crest of the hill it still lingers in what looks to be ladles of soup-like webs clinging tenaciously to the lowlands.

"We could definitely get up it if we went through the farm," says Wen.

"It does look like that doesn't it?"

"There's even a path in the bracken up to the top look."

"They'll be in though because presumably that was them in the Range Rover which passed us."

"What can they do? Turf us off their land... if they see us?"

"They're bound to see us, and I'd rather not trespass if at all possible. Let's have a look this way first."

...Admirable was the march to Red-Hill-Hall, as the men of Albion set out for the house of King Grim-Gaze with host, battalion and company under the leadership of their chieftains.

From the north came Connor Cruel-Crest and his host.

"Hail, mighty warrior: bright bannered bearer of the thunderbolt," said Father Fish, lolloping alongside Connor's company on foot, "by the time the men of Albion cross into foreign bounds you are a distance of three nights and three days in advance over many a ford, what then should hinder the Champion's Portion of Red-Hill-Hall being yours?"

Said Connor Cruel-Crest, "Why, if it isn't that lackey Fish Face, the unpaid fool of King Grim-Gaze," he laughed out loud and his company set up a shout and raised their spears.

127

"Truly, the Champion's Portion of the house I built is not that of a fool's house," smiled Father Fish, "belonging to it is a cauldron full of generous wine and a seven year old boar; since it was small nothing has entered its lips but fine meal in springtime, curds in summer, the kernel of nuts in autumn and beef broth in winter, indeed, the Champion's Portion of Red-Hill-Hall is well worth contesting; if it be yours then the Championship of Albion also will be yours forever."

Connor Cruel-Crest looked the fish man up and down.

Said Father Fish, "Since you are the bravest hero amongst the men of Albion, it is but just to give it to you, and so do I wish it."

"By the god of my clan," shouted Connor Cruel-Crest, "his head shall he lose, whosoever comes to contest it with me!"

Father Fish laughed at that, for it pleased him right well...

...So together we set off into the field and down the slope which leads to the left of the hill. We have not gone far when Wen, who has sort of marched off ahead, stops and turns back to me and in a accusatory manner proclaims,

"There is a llama in the next field!"

I smile nonchalantly, determined not to fall for that one,

"There cannot be a llama in the next field Wen, because we are in the North Yorkshire Moorlands and not the Mountains of Peru."

Still some distance ahead, Wen turns back to look into the field and then back to me and says,

"Not only is there very definitely a llama in the next field. It is now looking directly at us."

"There cannot be a llama..." I start to again remonstrate but then I catch up to Wen and look into the next field... at the llama, which appears to be waiting for us. "It appears to be waiting for us." Wen shrugs, turns and sets off down the slope toward the llama.

"Better not keep it waiting too long."

"What?"

"It may have a message for us."

...Poor Ben. It was all going so well...

...From the south came Long-Horn O'Leary and his host.

"Hail, the flame-hot hammerer: wielder of the red mallet," said Father Fish as he lolloped alongside O'Leary's company on foot. "When the men of Albion return from foreign lands you protect their rear so that an assailant may not spring past you, nor over you, what then should prevent the Champion's Portion of Red-Hill-Hall being yours?"

Said Long-Horn O'Leary, "Why, if it isn't that dullard Fish Face, come to pester me with his eccentric wit," he laughed aloud and his company set up a roar and raised their swords.

"Truly, the Champion's Portion of the house I built is not that of a dullard's house," smiled Father Fish, "belonging to it are five score cakes of wheat cooked in honey, and a cow-lord full seven years old; since it was a calf neither heather nor twig-tops have entered its lips, nothing but sweet milk and herbs, meadow-hay and corn, indeed, the Champion's Portion of Red-Hill-Hall is well worth contesting, for if it be yours then the Championship of Albion also will be yours forever."

Long-Horn O'Leary eyed the fish man warily.

Said Father Fish, "Since you are the finest hero amongst the men of Albion, it is just that it be yours, and so do I wish it."

"By the god of my clan," shouted Long-Horn O'Leary, "his head shall he lose whosoever comes to contest it with me!"

Father Fish laughed at that, for it pleased him right well...

If I am consciously following a woman who is about to engage a llama in conversation, which I certainly appear to be, it does not impinge too negatively upon my thought processes. To be perfectly honest I am more interested in the reaction of the llama. Will it turn and run like sheep do? If it is going to turn and run it is not showing any visible signs of doing so yet and Wen is within thirty or so yards of it now and closing with considerable purpose. Albeit there is a gate barring the exit from this field and the entrance into the next so she will have to slow down to get beyond that.

At about this point I also notice that there is a family of horses to the left of the gate which had previously been shielded by tree cover. A mare and two young foals. They are a lovely deep, shiny chestnut colour. They too are watching the scene unfold with an inordinate amount of interest and they too show no signs of bolting. It strikes me that the meeting between Livingstone and Stanley could not have been more fraught with impending tension and uncertainty.

Thankfully, Wen does slow down and stop when she reaches the gate, resting her hand upon it and taking a much needed breather. The llama has not moved a muscle. Not one, and has watched Wen's progress, and now mine, to the gate with something that can only be described as mild curiosity.

I too am a little out of breath so I sit on one of the cross slats of the fence that runs to the gate, a little to the right of Wen and the horses who are sidling towards her for a nosy.

Wen is far too intent on our friend the llama, who I suddenly remember is called Lammas, to notice the now rapid approach of one of the foals, until that is it starts to nibble her ear. She yelps and moves towards me past the gate.

"Ow, that hurt!"

"I think they want you to go into the other field," I laugh.

"Give us a hand then."

I help Wen over the fence into the llama's field and then follow. It is definitely the llama's field. He has still not budged. And as Wen advances to within no more than four feet of him he edges a little closer as if to say, "There and no further".

"Yeahs, you're beautiful aren't you?" says Wen to the llama.

Now llamas don't understand English, obviously, but as surely as I am sitting here typing this, he does begin to preen when Wen complements him on his beauty. So I am thinking, well he has maybe picked up on the tone in the vibration of Wen's voice and is responding to that. His keepers probably do that type of thing all the time... when they are about to feed him.

"I bet you know the way to the top of Our Sacred Hill don't you, beautiful?"

Lammas nods. Without a word of a lie, Lammas the llama nods an affirmative to a direct question. Okay, so Wen was also nodding, and so he could just have been copying her. Llama, see, llama do and all that.

"Which way is it then, gorgeous?"

Lammas turns his head... and looks... and nods to the left.

"...Which way?"

Lammas repeats the look... and the nod... to the left. Now you know Wen by now so it is highly likely that she asked three times and got three exactly similar responses and this is indeed what she insists happened. But, well perhaps I had buried my head in my hands in disbelief at this point or perhaps... because, well, for whatever reason, I was not paying close enough attention. I don't know, but personally I only heard and saw two, and not three, questions and responses. But either which way it is still not something that really ought to be happening in Yorkshire or Peru... or anywhere else for that matter.

But what are you supposed to do if a llama has given you directions on how to get up a Sacred Hill? Ask any Tibetan Buddhist... you follow them. Which is precisely what we do.

Well, eventually that is what we do if not actually straight away. Initially, to our eternal shame, we fiddle about ruling out every other possible avenue of approach before reluctantly admitting that Lammas was probably right after all.

It means climbing back up the gentle slope of the first field to where we had first seen the Hill. This time though when we look at the gateway to the farm we see a sign. It reads: "Beware farm vehicles". Now if there is a sign warning the general public to be wary of farm vehicles, it must mean that the general public are allowed to walk through the farm. Obvious really.

"Why didn't we see that sign before?"

"It might not have been there."

"Yeah, and llamas might talk..."

Realising the enormity of what Wen has just said, we walk through the farm-yard in silence. Not only are there no farm vehicles to be seen. There is no sign of life at all... farm-life or otherwise. But what is more, upon reaching the other side of the ghost-farm... we have a clear run up to the crest of Blakey Topping.

"Woo-hoo!"

BRIG'S LAY

Lay me down beneath an Iron Sky
In the centred stillness of a Dragon-Eye...
And let sweet-odorous heather be my pall
On a speaking hill where angel-feathers fall...
With earth beneath my skin and sky above
I shall await, in silence, the descent of Love.

Blakey Topping, August 2013

Chapter Eight
SIMPLE, SIMEON

"...This is the answer to all our questions.
This, the prodigal come home to rest..."
Endless Round

The Presentation in the Temple.

"What's the difference between a shadow and a ghost?"

"Really, Wen, you do ask the most perplexing questions."

"Oh, and you don't?"

"Well, I usually give you at least some warning."

"You don't know..."

"I don't know, no, but I am going to have a stab at it. The shadow shows the Son how and the ghost is the Earth made Divine again."

"That's not at all bad for a fake Filid."

...As the men of Albion entered the mead house in Red-Hill-Hall that Father Fish built, each hero occupied a couch and sat his young braves round him.

While the feast was being prepared the musicians and players of King Grim-Gaze performed their arts.

Father Fish spread the table with its savouries before he withdrew to his sun bower, unobserved...

"You are aware that 'fake' derives from fakir and that the fakirs are masters of the art of mind over matter..."

"That's my Don, always happy to turn an insult into a compliment even though fake doesn't actually derive from fakir at all."

We are on the vacation proper and the Silver-Bullet is heading this way and that along the 'A' and 'B' roads of North Yorkshire. There are draw-backs to not having a properly conceived plan. I pick up the road map in an attempt to put some direction back into proceedings and that is when we find Thornton-Le-Dale...

Wen sees the Congress Stone first off and whilst we are 'humming' and 'hawing' about whether or not to stop, we skirt past the churched hillock which more or less clinches it although there is also the small matter of the scarecrows...

We are both conscious, I think, that today should be a landscape day but churches like this... they simply demand exploration. And boy, are we ever glad that we stopped.

It would have been all too easy to press on, make a mental note to return at some point and never get around to it. I still shudder to think about the consequences if we had done that...

...As the spencers rose to serve the food, the charioteer of Connor Cruel-Crest stood up and addressed the king.

"O Far Seeing One," he said, "many are the feats of Connor; majestic and commanding his gait, clashing swords he brings together, and in front of them he strides in glory to destroy all before him; in battles of blood, the pride of armies he hews, mowing down hosts of his foe-men; ever hostile is his hand, and many the mighty victories he has scored for Albion. Do you assign to Connor the Champion's Portion, he alone is entitled to it before all the other heroes of Albion?"

"That is not so!" cried the charioteer of Long-Horn O'Leary, leaping to his feet. "To O'Leary should the Champion's Portion be assigned, he alone before any other man of Albion is deserving of it: sprung from loins that are royal, fostered in warrior virtues; more famous than all Albion's heroes, the guardian of every ford-way; big is his shield, it protects from wounds, his friends he defends from their foe-men; by O'Leary's hand are they held, equal in every strength, all noble."

Father Fish called down from his sun bower, "The Champion's Portion of Red-Hill-Hall is not that of a fool's or a dullard's house, who do you prefer for valour?"

Whereupon the whole assembly ran for their shields and seized their weapons: within the space of a gnat's eye-blink the hall was aflame with the clash of sword edge and spear point, and the floor became a white sheet of shield enamel.

Said Father Fish from his sun bower,

"Why, 'tis a bad look-out tonight and no mistake!"

...Apart from anything else, Thornton-le-Dale is the quintessential English village but today, upon this day of days, it also happens to be festooned with scarecrows! A scarecrow festival!

Now if you had suggested to me at the outset of our little jaunt that there were nowadays such things as scarecrow festivals, I would have shrugged your suggestion aside with a haughty wave of the hand and a pronounced snort... Pah! Scare-crow festival?

But, well, here we are, bang smack in the middle of one and what is more we are enjoying it immensely. These days, they are not real scare-crows, not your straw-man with black coat and topper looking, for all the world like a derelict Christ on his crossed wooden support.

Country magic according to Robert Graves... They never were meant to scare the crows, which is just as well because the crows usually line the horizontal cross beam anyway. A fertility charm positioned in the fields: now why do you suppose a simple wooden cross, dressed as a man could be regarded as a symbol of fertility?

But as I said, these are not real scare-crows more dummies really, in different guises, or guys, indeed, more like your "penny for the guy", guys... but positioned at various points in the village and in various poses...

So there is an Army-crow in camouflage combats crouching with mortar on shoulder behind a tree... which Wen sees and I manage to miss completely... must be the camouflage...

There is a Vamp-crow replete with extended cigarette holder soliciting attention on the bridge which frames the picturesque, thatched cottage...

There is even a White-Rabbit-crow along with an Alice-crow enjoying their tea party on the pavement in the centre of the village shops...

I mean, how many clues do we really need?

At least one more. On our way up to the churched hillock which turns out to be an All Saints we pass a John-the-Baptist-crow and a Humpty-Dumpty-crow.

I kid you not.

There is actually a John-the-Baptist-crow expertly positioned in the village stream, emerging from the waters exhorting his wayward flock... to turn within.

As you can imagine, such picture language has my head in something of a spin but I am still trying to keep the lid on my excitement as we approach the churched hillock.

As a now highly experienced church-tapper of over six months standing, I know only too well that if you let your expectations run away with you it invariably ends in disappointment...

...King Grim-Gaze, the slug-man, struck the silver sceptre that was in his hand against the bronze pillar of his couch three times, and by the third stroke, the combatants had let drop their hands to their sides.

"I restrain you, men of Albion, lest your mien be the paler: your shields are likely to be splintered in the attack for that to which you have not yet attained. My feast has to be celebrated and my wish is to divide the Champion's Portion amongst the host and to decide with reference to it according to the will of Maeve, she whose mouth is sweet, and who resides in Tower Hill-Fort. Tomorrow, the heroes shall ride there for judgement, enjoy the food and ale before you, and let rivalry be put aside until the feast is over."

So did the men of Albion return to their seats round the fire, to make light of the night, long into the dawn of morning.

...Although we did not yet realise, how could we? This particular revelation had already started earlier in the morning when we took a look

137

at St Gregory's of Cropton. It is a Gregory and not a St George even though both Wen and I read the sign pointing it out as George and even though the information board for the hillfort which stands behind it has... St George.

More confirmation, if it were needed, about the nature of perception. Curiously enough though, there does just happen to be a rather gorgeous stained glass depiction of St George in this particular Church.

And I know... a hillfort in the village where we are staying! And here we are merrily traipsing across the country-side looking for them. We had checked out the Fort on the first night, when the church was shut and as is becoming the norm for such jaunts all the familiar 'catchphrases' were there... the eerie sense of presence, the stunning prospects, the sense of otherworldly peace... So, who lives on a hill like this?

...Circles upon circles... the ripples spread across the surface of the pond. Here and there a solitary fish rises, a denizen of one world breaching the barrier to reach into another, capturing the midges that fly in the dusk. On the horizon, flashes of lightning signal the approaching storm. The busy life of the castle seems to hang in the air like the smoke from the cooking fires.

He throws another pebble in the pond and watches the wider circles swallow the smaller and become one. He wipes his nose on the coarse, brown sleeve. Tears have streaked through the dirt on his face; the beating was harsh for one so small. The Ostler is a big man. The Smith had stopped it. He had run away.

The grass is high, a purple mist of wildflowers, the spreading branches of the elder a shield from angry eyes. It wasn't his fault. He didn't ask for it. Hadn't even known he was different. How could he? His world was as it was... He could not see it was not the same world others saw. Heard... Felt...

He scared them. He knew things. He was Fey...

He had talked to the soldier. They had come from far away, marching across the hill with their sharp swords and short kilts, shiny metal at their breast and sun dark skin. One was kind, let him share their fire and told him about their home, far beyond Rome. The other soldiers did not seem to see him.

He had learned from the wise woman who muttered to herself about the herbs and the berries she gathered from summer trees when the snow lay on the ground. He had seen the blue-painted faces of the Small Ones as they camped on the hilltop.

The others said there was no-one there. But he knew... he could see them.

The Ostler was afraid... They were all afraid except the Smith.

So they called him mad... Fey... Fool... and threw scraps to him in the Hall. They let him sleep with the horses in the warm, sweet hay.

He was no fool. Just alone in a world the others could not see...

...The next day Connor Cruel-Crest and Long-Horn O'Leary met at the stables of King Grim-Gaze the slug-man.

"Let our horses be brought and our chariot's yoked," said O'Leary.

"There will be little profit for you in that," said Connor. "By the men of Albion, the clumsiness of your horses is renowned, as is the unsteadiness of your going and turnabout."

"And your chariot's movement is so heavy that it's two wheels raise turf on both sides," said O'Leary, "so that for a year after your passing the track is still recognisable to the men of Albion."

"Put not on me the precedence of kings until I have fared before the Champions of Albion in woods and confines," cried Connor as he stepped into his chariot.

"Put not on me the precedence of kings until I have nimbly

crossed fords and outstripped the Champions of Albion," cried O'Leary stepping into his chariot...

...He watched two figures striding across the hilltop. A man and woman laughing in the dusk. They were talking. He could hear their voices, but the words were strange. The woman stopped and picked up a feather, holding it out to the man. They stopped and looked at it.

He knew. It was an owl. The birds too saw things other eyes did not see. The man was tall and slender, carrying a leather pouch across his shoulder. All in black, tight like a knight's gambeson. She was small, brightly coloured, her hair like flame catching the last of the light.

He liked their laughter. It warmed the coldness around him. He watched as they walked on. She looked over and met his eyes. She smiled at him. He could see the castle lights through her. But she saw him and she smiled...

He watches the surface of the pond as the ripples merge one into the other... like time.

...So the heroes of Albion set out for Tower Hill-Fort: through the Gap-of-the-Watch, over the Plain-of-Two-Forks, across the Ford-of-the-Morrigan into the Rowan-Meadow-of-the-Two-Oxen by the Meeting-of-the-Four-Ways they drove before a dim, dark, heavy mist overtook them...

...The churchyard of St Greg's has a fake Congress Stone but fake or not the symbolism is still valid. A line of light linking the worlds. It also has a basilica-shaped chancel which again, though late, still works, yet again proving that it is possible to renovate and preserve when one is attuned.

The stained glass is another example.

It is late but beautiful and totally in keeping with the quiet unassuming spirit of the place. Enough to make one's heart sing...

The readings here, perhaps unsurprisingly in the circumstances, proved to be eye-opening, literally. Without going too deeply into a textural analysis what we were told is that salvation is a perception or rather, as the texts have it... a salve for the eyes.

Now, it would be easy to translate 'salve' as balm and that would obviously ruin the argument... or maybe not. I for one am, and always have been, quite happy to be seen as 'balmy'. Anyway, the point is that if salvation is a perception, then the notion of an outside agency, that is, a saviour, becomes all but defunct. Jesus, save us? Save your selves... people... or salve your eyes...

"...The kingdom is like a person who sowed good seed. His enemies came at night and sowed weeds among the good seed, but that person refused to dig up the seeds saying instead, "On the day of the harvest the weeds will become conspicuous.""

The Living One

"...Jesus saith unto her, Woman, why weepest thou? Whom seekest thou? She supposing him to be the Gardener saith unto him, "Sir, if thou have borne him hence, tell me where thou hast laid him, and I will take him away." Jesus saith unto her, "Mary". She turned herself and saith unto him... "Rabboni"; which is to say, "Master!""

St John 20: 15-16

"I have always been perplexed by that passage," says Wen. "Is it normal not to recognise one's beloved?"

"As an indication of the transformational effect of the rising though it works beautifully."

"She only recognises him through the voice."

"Well, he is supposed to be the Word."

""She turned herself" is a curious phrase don't you think?"

"It may indicate that the beloved is also transformed."

"Through what though?"

"Through understanding."

"Yes, through understanding."

In Tower Hill-Fort, Very-White of the Clear-Sight sat in meditation, "Mother," she said, "I see a chariot coming over the plain."

"Describe it," said Sweet-Mouthed Maeve.

Said Very-White, "Truly, I see horses pulling the chariot:

> two stormy dappled greys
> alike in colour and shape;
> nostrils wide
> heads erect
> ears pricked;
> manes flowing
> of full slim-girth
> their tails curled;
> galloping side by side
> bounding apace
> they career along.

> A chariot of fine wood,
> the high frame's wicker-work
> creaks above its two black wheels:
> its curved yoke is silver mounted.

> In the chariot
> a dark, melancholy man:
> his eyebrows jet
> his face pale
> cheeks ruddy;

142

his blue mantle is
held across the chest
by a salmon brooch.

A three-pronged javelin
gleams from his shoulder.

An awning of bird plumage
waves from his chariot frame...

...Before we enter the church proper we have a couple more clues to fathom. The first one takes the form of an empty manger tied to the gate post. Initially this one does not actually mean anything to me at all I have to say. Even in the context of a scarecrow festival it fails to sound any horns as our new-old saying would have it.

"So where's the baby?"

The second one has Wen in a bit of a spin but only because she believes it to be a real owl and starts talking to it!

There is a plastic owl in the awning of the church porch which we eventually work out is to stop the house martins from nesting in there!

"I recognise that man," said Maeve,

"An ocean fury:
a whale that rages in the crash of battle,
like the back-stroke of waves against the land;

in face a man
in mien a hero

143

in heart a dragon;
swift, as the speckled trout
on sand stone is cut, the red
hand of Connor Cruel-Crest...

...The first clue does eventually start to make sense to me though and when it does it becomes an integral part of one of the most astounding realisations I have yet experienced. But I do not actually get there until I have considered the Simeon window, which stands brazen as you like, proclaiming its message to the world in the chancel of All Saints, Thornton-le-Dale.

It is to be sure a fine window in its own right. It is beautifully realised and the colour scheme is nothing less than exquisite. The green and the blue of the two figures alternate from high to low between the robes and the halos and that alone would have saved us a lot of mental angst last time out if we had come across it then.

Ostensibly, the window by Henry Holiday shows the Virgin in the left light as we look at it, with the temple offering of two turtle doves in a wooden cage... and already I am beginning to get excited. Because what the artist has actually depicted are two white doves... a temple offering of two white doves... they are not turtle doves at all... and they are certainly not pigeons. Although, if the artist responsible wanted a let-out he could possibly argue that they are in fact white pigeons.

Very clever, Mr Holiday... Always cover your back.

Now, why do you suppose he would do that?

The other exciting thing about the left light is that the Virgin depicted there is, well, shall we say, 'a lady of a certain age?' She is certainly not a woman, or young girl of the age that the Virgin is purported to be at this time. It has to be the Virgin though because the right light as we look at it depicts Simeon, the High Priest who received the 'Christ-Child' before giving up the Ghost... in perfect peace.

Oh, Mr Holiday... your window is rapidly advancing to the head

144

of the leading group of all time genius windows!

The coup-de-grace of this particular window though is the central roundel which spans the two lights. In the central roundel is a floating head with the moniker... JOHN... beneath...

Inevitably, my subconscious gets there first and it is all I can do to prevent myself sinking to my knees... weeping. I manage to stifle a sob whilst my mind races with the possibilities and enormities of what I am looking at. I glance over my shoulder to check that I am still here... and sure enough Wen has taken up position at the lectern and is reading the passage from St. Luke which purportedly relates to the Window. Wen, as you by now know, is clever like that...

I am right then... it is Luke and not John. My knees are about to start buckling again, so I take one last lingering look at the window and head back into the nave, more to collect my thoughts than anything else...

At this point, a family with a little girl enter the church and the little girl runs to the font and places a Baby-Jesus-crow on its lid with exquisite delicacy, looks longingly at it with the pride of an artist who does not want to let go, and then, at the bequest of her insistent mother she turns and runs from the church... and suddenly, like the collapsing kaleidoscope of time, I understand... everything...

"Everything?"

"Yes, everything..."

"For example..."

"For example, I now understand that the little girl has just returned the baby..."

"Which baby?"

"The baby that was thrown out..."

"...with the bath-water."

...Said Very-White, "It is but a drop before a shower:
I see another chariot coming over the plain."

"Describe it," said Sweet-Mouthed Maeve.

Said Very-White, "I see the
horses pulling the chariot:

two fiery, spirited bays of
great strength and power;
wide of hoof, with
sweat spittled chests
and curbed jaws;

high mettled their
broad foreheads
their manes curled;
swift and smooth,
they run a tumultuous course
of wild and dashing pace.

A chariot of fine wood,
its wicker-work new and freshly spruced,
having two wheels of bronze;
its pole bright with gold mountings.

In the chariot a man
much freckled,
his hair long and curly:
his tresses tri-hued;
brown at root
red in mass with
tips corn yellow.

About his body
a crimson tunic
striped gold.

A shield alongside
yellow bossed
edged in bronze.

From his wrist shoots
a shining broad sword.

A grandly moving billow
waves from his chariot frame...

I know now why the parentheses of St Luke's 'Grand Supposition' were so offensive. I had wondered if it is the only example of their use. They are there to signal an interpolation. And when I have twigged that I start to look for more. And they are legion...

Luke 1:15 "... even from his mother's womb..." This is neither possible nor necessary and, within the strictures of the tradition to which it purportedly relates, it never happens. Never has done... and never will do. So why is it there? It is Pauline... It is Paul who is specifically concerned with this notion of the Son of God'. The 'prophet' himself never uses such terminology, he talks in terms only of Father and of Son. Heavenly Father and Earthly Son to give them their correct and precise terminology...

Luke 3:22 "... a voice from heaven..."

"...The voice from heaven?"

"Is the Priest's voice, and in the 'true' tradition, only the Priest can confer the Holy Ghost."

"The Priest who is Satan?"

"Not quite, the Priest who *plays* the Satan but who is actually Lucifer, which means 'the bearer of light in the darkness.'"

"So, if John doesn't have the Holy Ghost from birth, and it can only be conferred on him by one who holds it, when is it conferred?"

"It is conferred on him by Simeon at *his* presentation in the temple."

147

"Can you prove any of this?"

"Of course not, but I can point to that window over there by way of confirmation that I am not the only person to have entertained such a notion. It shows The Light of the World carrying the Cross of John the Baptist."

Twin-Suns.

Chapter Nine
A KNOBBED CLUB

"...Let your love fly like a bird on the wing
Let your love bind you to all living things..."
The Bellamy Brothers.

Hairy Wild Man

...We wonder about the Bride Stones...

Brig as in high presumably...

Weathered sandstone blocks that once formed the Jurassic sea-bed over a million years ago and which today stand high in ancient woodland that has survived since the Iron Age. It is probably going to be difficult to be disappointed... and we are not.

Given distance and the right angle, the sandstone blocks look like nothing less than giant heads emerging from the hills to take a look around.

And in such a landscape it is easy to imagine a settlement of sorts.

Even easier when from the top of one of the heads we can both see and hear the folk lounging on top of a cave across the tree lined valley. Our nuclear family show us the way to get there. Their dysfunction punctures the deep silence with little explosions of sound like word bombs.

From the cave opposite, our initial viewpoint, I can see spear-clad figures on all the giant heads and the feeling grows that someone really ought to film up here...

...“I recognise that man,”
said Maeve, “a wolf among cattle,
in battle after battle,
head upon head he heaps;

through furious foe,
he leaps like a flame,
his name the call to rout;
eager for fray, the sword
of Long-Horn O'Leary
...is a raven to prey.”

...Dusk falls quickly as the mists in autumn and here in the sheltered valley the light is fading.

The thin grass is wet and dew-cold as they alight from their ponies, setting them to graze and drink from the wide, slow moving stream.

They leave the sheepskins over the ponies' backs.

It will be cold tonight. The sky is clear and a smell of frost is in the air.

Those who are to remain set camp, kindling a small blaze...

...We sheltered just in time for the rain is now pitter-pattering on the roof of our rock-house...

"So why are there two different genealogies for the Christ-Child?"

"One of them is John's."

"But which is which?"

"Jesus descends from Solomon. John, not unsurprisingly, perhaps, descends from Nathan. They tell you that they're cousins, one only has to substitute Zacharias for Joseph..."

"So why does John's line go all the way back to God whilst Jesus' only goes forwards from Abraham."

"In order to indicate that the line of light is passed by John as initiator, and also to emphasise the link between the Christ sacrament and that of Melchizedek, the initiator of Abraham."

"You seem to have it all worked out."

"It's all in there... but it has been tampered with although not too drastically."

"Just enough to make one have to work."

"Well, we shouldn't decry a little work. It's good for the soul after all."

...They cannot ride the last stretch of their journey, the hill before them is steep, the path narrow and strewn with rocks.

He looks back at his companions and smiles grimly. They are clever, the Old Ones.

Their place is high above the valley, an island between deep gullies and tumbling streams, well protected.

This is the only way... and any who attempt it could be picked off one by one...

"How should these mighty
men of war be greeted?"
said Very-White...

Said Sweet-Mouthed Maeve,
"Women to meet them,
bonnie, full-breasted and bare,
with strong ale, well malted,
their food, not scanty but fare."

..."There is one thing troubling me," says Wen.

"Which is?"

"The child in the arms of Simeon has a cross in his halo..."

"Hmm..."

"Well isn't a cross in the halo supposed to be indicative of Christ, who died on the cross?"

"A cross in the halo may be indicative of Christ who died on the cross, or in this particular case who will die on the cross, it may not... but in the halo of the child in Simeon's arms, I don't see any cross at all."

"What then do you see?"

"I see three golden rays of light."

"Which is indicative of?"
"The Holy Trinity."

...But that is not their way, nor is he an attacker.

He, chieftain though he is, mighty in arms and father of many, tonight he is a supplicant.

He studies the calm, pale face of the Weaver. Tall, slender, with that faraway look in his eyes... eyes that see little of the world, yet see into Beyond. They meet his and the Chieftain looks away... he cannot hold that gaze, not even he. It sees too much.

It sees his soul and the lies there...

...So the heroes of Albion
were bathed, fed and entertained,
each in their separate compartments.

When sated and fully rested, Very-White
went to each of them in turn
in order to discover
the reason for their visit.

She returned to Maeve and said,
"The men of Albion are contending
over the Champion's Portion in the mead house
of King Grim-Gaze the slug-man.

They have agreed to abide
by your judgement in the matter."...

Maeve's honeyed lips curved

153

into an inscrutable smile.

"Have them perform the wheel feat
of the youths in the morning," she said.

..."As we're in speculative mode..."

"It's the rain. It does that!"

"Well, given that on this reading of the tradition we are placing emphasis on the fact that it is John who has an uncle called Joseph..."

"I'm not going to like this am I?"

"That depends on how much you like worms."

"Donald Sams...I hate you! But go on."

"It could have been John's feet that walked these ancient shores..."

"The Light of the World in the Heart of Albion..."

...No matter.

Tonight would be the last time.

His was the price of Knowledge.

They start towards the hill, climbing the rugged, slippery path.

Even for him, for his men, used to the desolate moors, the way is difficult. And it is doubly hard here, on this border between the worlds.

Ahead, a single boulder is outlined in the faint light, blocking the path. As he approaches it moves, standing... laughing toothlessly at their fear...

The following morning the men of Albion were woken early and taken to a hall in which youths were performing the wheel feat.

First Long-Horn O'Leary seized the wheel, he threw it in the air and it reached in height the ridge pole of the hall; the youths in the hall laughed and jeered at his effort but O'Leary heard their reaction as cheers and was elated.

Then Connor Cruel-Crest seized the wheel, he threw it in the air and it reached in height the ridge pole of the hall; the youths in the hall cheered and applauded his effort but Connor heard their reaction as jeers and was dejected.

Said Sweet-Mouthed Maeve to Very-White, "To whom do you think we should award the Champion's Portion of Albion?"

...Wild hair, grey and crowned with dead heather hangs down across the pendulous, naked breasts, wrinkled as weather-worn bark.

The Old One leans on a staff, more for effect, he feels, than necessity.

He waits, silent, for the Old One to speak.

She does not.

She simply looks on, raking each with her eyes, reading them one after the other... until she meets those of the fey one...

"It is difficult for me to decide," said Very-White, "for there is nothing to choose between the two of them."

Said Sweet-Mouthed Maeve, " O my child, there is no difficulty, for in truth, Long-Horn O'Leary, and Connor of the Cruel-Crest are different as white and red gold."

...She beckons and he approaches, kneeling before her.

She takes the alabaster hands in hers, turning them over, tracing their lines and nodding as the delicate fingers hold themselves open to her gaze. There is something silent between them as she traces the pale cheek with a long, blackened claw, leaving the dark trail of blood behind it.

He does not flinch. Accepting...

She binds the pale hands, passing the cord around his neck, haltering him like a horse.

He does not move until she jerks him to his feet.

Then he waits...

...So Long-Horn O'Leary was taken into the presence of the one whose mouth is sweet: "Welcome," said Maeve, "in preference to Connor Cruel-Crest, I assign to you a cup of gold with a bird chased in silver on its bottom. Take it with you as a token of award. No one else is to see it until, at the days end, you are in the mead hall of king Grim-Gaze.

When the Champion's Portion is exhibited among the men of Albion, then shall you bring out the cup in their presence and none of them will dispute further with you."

Then the cup with its full of luscious mead was given to O'Leary, and he downed the contents in a draught.

"Having tasted the mead of kings," said Maeve, "I wish that you may enjoy it a hundred years at the head of all the men of Albion."

...The Chieftain watches shuddering and she cackles, delighting in his fear. There is power here. And it is hers.

She draws herself up to her full height and strikes the flint-shod staff against the stone beneath her feet.

Sparks fly... once... twice... three times...

An eldritch cry escapes her lips, echoing eerily through the darkened vale.

His men draw back. Only he and the bound one remain.

The Old One pulls the rope and they begin the ascent...

Then Connor Cruel-Crest came before the one whose mouth is sweet.

"Welcome," said Maeve. "In preference to Long-Horn O'Leary, I assign to you a cup of silver with a bird chased in gold on its bottom. Take it with you as a token of award. No one else is to see it until, at the days end, you are in the mead hall of king Grim-Gaze.

When the Champion's Portion is exhibited among the men of Albion, then shall you bring out the cup in their presence and none of them will dispute further with you."

So the cup with its full of luscious mead was given to Connor, and he downed the contents in a draught.

"Having tasted the mead of kings," said Maeve, "I wish that you may enjoy it a hundred years at the head of all the men of Albion."

...The ropes bite his skin.

His hands are soft, white, unblemished. He is neither warrior nor farmer. It is his to see and to spin the lays of learning.

His gift is other than the rest, his body made for gentleness and dreaming. He does not sing at the feast nor amuse his Chieftain on a winter night.

He Knows... he Sees... he Weaves the Words.

He follows the Old One. He could escape her grip, but he submits. He serves the clan and his life is theirs.

Tonight he is the price paid, the gift to the gods...

...In the mead house of Grim-Gaze, King of the Slug-Men, the Heroes of Albion ceased their boastings, the ladder-vat of ale was filled for them, and the spencers came to serve the Champion's Portion.

Father Fish slipped out of the mead house unnoticed.

Connor Cruel-Crest stood and lifted on high the silver cup, with the bird chased in gold on the bottom, given to him by Sweet-Mouthed Maeve, "The Champion's Portion is mine," he said, "and none of the men of Albion may contest it with me."

"That is not so," said Long-Horn O'Leary, raising his own cup which was gold with a bird chased in silver on the bottom. "From the difference in the tokens which Maeve gave to us it is clear that the Champion's Portion belongs to me alone."

In the silence which had fallen on the company, a loud wailing from without the mead house could be heard by all those present.

...His eyes watch the dirty, cracked heels of the bare feet before him on the path, skipping up the hillside like a child, ancient and ever-young.

Light flares to the south, high on a rock... a strange, susurrating whisper echoes through the valley, winding its way like a mist-wraith through the bracken.

Another light appears to the north. It is a deeper sound, like a heart beating slow and steady. The sounds join, woven in a single note like blood rushing through the veins.

The lights remain. Another joins them, another still, alternating, one after another, north and south. With each flare of fire a new sound, strange ululations and whispers, cries and the call of the hawk in the morning... the first cry of a babe and the sighing of the last breath...

Into the house that Father Fish built strode a big, uncouth fellow of un-surpassing ugliness.

Twice the height of any of the men of Albion was the horrible mantle about him and his hair was like a great spreading bush the size of a winter shed, under which thirty bullocks could easily find shelter. He had ravenous yellow eyes the size of an ox vat, which bulged from his head, and each of his fingers were the width of any normal man's wrist.

In his left hand he carried a block, a burden for twenty yoke of oxen, and in his right, an axe weighing a hundred and fifty molten masses of metal.

Its handle required a plough team of six to move it, and its edge was of a sharpness to slice a hair blown by the wind...

...Across the valley a warp of light is woven, and the weft of life completes the weaving with sound. He is walking through the body of the earth, hearing life and death, feeling it in his bones... the rhythm of his own heart changing its tempo to join the dancing sounds.

He is lifted out of himself...

He sees the line of dark blood like a tear falling on his cheek...

He sees the slight frame stumbling up the rocky path behind the Old One.

Behind him he reads fear in his Chieftain, in line and movement... and a pride that seeks to hide it.

As they reach the plateau a final fire blazes... a pyramid of flame, like to the hills of home.

From a cave behind the blaze a great drum beats, pinning the sound in the valley.

Pinning his soul there with its weight...

...He strode across the hall and stood by the fork-beam of the fire.

"Is the hall lacking in size that you seek to hog the fire with your bulk?" asked King Grim-Gaze. "You are as a shadow cast across the sun."

You need have no fear of my shadow," rumbled the carle, "I possess the capacity to enlighten the whole household with this blaze behind me but tonight that is not my purpose."

"Then what is your purpose?" asked King Grim-Gaze.

"I have a covenant to make," said the clod-hopper, "for neither in Africa nor Asia, nor yet throughout the whole of Europe have I found the man to do me fair play regarding it: since the men of Albion excel all the folk of those lands for strength, prowess and valour, I hope to find me one among you to fulfil it."

"What then is this covenant which no one has so far met?" said King Grim-Gaze.

The foul fellow cast down the block into the middle of the hall and brandished his mighty axe. "Whoever agrees to allow me to cut off his head with my axe tonight, I will grant him the same with regard to my own head on the morrow and along with it the Championship of Albion."

"By the god of my tribe," said Connor Cruel-Crest, "death is not such a pleasant prospect, if the man killed tonight returns to attack you on the morrow," he lowered his cup and sat down.

"By the god of my tribe," said Long-Horn O'Leary, "the man able to return on the morrow after suffering death the previous night would leave no man alive in Albion," he lowered his cup and sat down.

"Sure then, is there no warrior here after these two?" roared the ogre surveying the mead house, with a piercing, jaundiced eye.

...The Old One turns, holding out her hand to the Chieftain.

He offers the treasures he has brought. She takes them, turning them over, in her hands... riches and beauties of the craftsman's art... then casts them aside, into the flames.

They seek no riches, these folk... only secrets...

The Chieftain pushes the fey one forward, he stumbles against the breast of the Old One and she catches him, strong hands hold him like a mother holds a babe.

She draws him to her, away from his Chieftain, smiling and nodding.

A wordless question... The fey one smiles acquiescence.

He is led away beyond the flame.

He has always known...

"Indeed there is," shouted Fat-Head, the son of Short-Neck, and he sprang into the middle of the mead house, "bend down you grizzly gawp, that I might cut off your head tonight and you to cut off mine tomorrow."

"But if that were my covenant I could have got it anywhere."

"Yet to you alone, it would seem, is given the power to be killed every night, and to avenge your death upon the following day."

"That's true," said the monstrous man, "I will agree to what you suggest." He bent down and put his neck across the block.

With that Fat-Head took the axe from the giant's hand; its two angles were a full seven feet apart on the stock, yet he struck at the hairy one's neck until his severed head lay at the base of the fork beam of the fire.

Straight away the unnatural hulk rose, recovered himself, clasped his head, block and axe to his breast, and made his exit from the mead hall with the blood still gurgling from his neck...

...Blood.... entrails... oil... and water...

Thick, choking smoke and scorched flesh.

Prophecy and answer...

161

The Chieftain departs. Satisfied. Alone.

High on the hill, beyond the flames, beyond the cave, the pale flesh is stripped.

The cords are cut...

Sound, heartbeat of earth, the sighing of air, the crackle of flame... resonating through the valley, across the high places, reaching a crescendo, a scream of the mother at birth.

He is lost in sound.

The next day, as the men of Albion watched Fat-Head to see whether he would shirk his covenant they saw a great dejection seize him, and some asked if they should start their keen.

Said Fat-Head, "It is true, my death is coming to me but I'd sooner my neck be broken than my word."

As night approached the carle came into the hall as before, "Where is Fat-Head," he said, "for the squat one has a covenant to keep."

"Here I am," said Fat-Head, rising from his seat.

"You're dull of speech tonight unhappy one," said the fiend, "greatly must you fear to die, yet I see that you have not shirked your fate."

Fat-Head went up to the swarthy chap and stretched his neck across the block but so big was its groove that his head reached only half-way.

"Stretch out your neck, wretch," roared the giant, lifting his mighty axe.

"Despatch me quickly, you keep me in torment," shouted Fat-Head.

"I cannot slay you, what with the size of the block coupled with the shortness of your scrawny neck," yelled back the fiend.

"I shall make my neck as long as the cranes above you," cried Fat-Head, and he stretched himself out so that a warrior's full grown foot would have fitted between any two of his ribs; his neck extended until his head reached the other side of the block.

The mighty man raised his axe till it reached the roof-tree of the hall; the creaking of the old hide that was about him and the crashing of the axe were as the loud noise of a wood, tempest tossed, in a night of storm, but the axe blade glided from the neck of Fat-Head as if it had been stone.

"Truly, the Championship of Albion to Fat-Head," shouted the carle, and he lifted the little fellow onto his shoulders."

"By the god of my Clan," laughed Fat-Head, from the giant's shoulders, as the two of them left the mead house, "his head shall he lose whosoever comes to contest it with me!"...

"Wen..."

"Now."

"I know now."

"What do you now know?"

"I know there is no real death, only the death of the personality."

"How do you know that?"

"It's that Latin phrase everybody makes such a fuss over."

"Et in Arcadia ego."

"That's the One..."

...The Old One washes him in the chill waters of the mountain stream, cleansing, purifying, bathing him like the babe he is... new born into a new life.

A Word-Weaver of the Valley...

The Word-Weave of the Whispering-Stones...

163

...Once outside the mead house, Father Fish and Little Nipper, Champions of the Crafty Folk, shifted into their own shape, and set off for Eden Dale.

Alongside them walked Grey-Sway: she was leading the white, black-maned cow, chosen by Father Fish as the price of his labour.

Our rainbow cow

A LITTLE BIT MORE
FOR ITINERANTS LIKE US...

THE GAZETTEER

There has to be a gazetteer, from precedent proceeding
To help you find the churches nine of which we have been reading.
By following the clues that hide within these cryptic pages
You'll find the beauty waiting there throughout the silent ages.
From sculpted heads to reredos, to walls by masters painted,
And musket balls within the walls man's history has tainted...
They all await the seeker's eye, their doors await your hand,
So journey with us yet awhile across this blessed land.

THE LADY'S SHADOW

A miracle awaited down a lost and lonely track,
After a mile of houseless field we'd thought of turning back.
A cross from old Atlantis seemed to stand beside the door
That bears the trace of moon and sun and ancient scars of war.
The jewelled windows tell the story of the Christmas saint
An orchestra of angels glow in mediaeval paint.

SILVER LIGHT

We'd searched a landscaped garden of a very stately school
In search of Watkins' line that runs from where the monarchs rule.
The windows were not stained, but etched, and in their silver light
A monumental archway and an eagle taking flight.
Upon the lectern waited an intriguing family tree
That held the clues to riddles left for those with eyes to see.

A VIRGIN'S BIRTH

While travelling to Windsor we were driving down a ley;
It seemed we ought to stop at all the churches on the way.
This tiny jewel caught our eye, with ORC-like bell and yew,
Inside we found twin dragons and examined George anew.
Four Holy Creatures carved in stone and Majesty above,
Beside the door a poem that distils the Word of Love.

AN ENGLISH SAINT

Beheaded on the altar steps the mediaeval saint
To whom this church is dedicated, watches now in paint
Beneath the leafy castle where a king sleeps in a cave
And Simeon keeps vigil from a window in the nave.
There is a sweetness in this place of hallowed ancient prayer
Just listen in the silence to the legends whispered there.

A MERE SHELL

The chairs arranged in circles, coming from the Table Round
Where revelations had been shown clear written on the ground.
With painted tombs of armoured knights it seemed a little odd
To get such confirmation in this holy house of God.
Baptismal shells abounded in the statues and the art
That point to new beginnings in the journey of the heart.

A CRYSTAL SPRING

There are giants in the stonework on the outside of this place
With every strange expression carved upon each sculpted face.
A sacred well lies close to hand where saints were wont to drink;
Yet more beheadings on the wall, the craftsmen made us think...
Both outer life and inner in symbolic form are shown
It only takes the 'eyes to see' before the way is known.

A PAINTED STORY

Our faces lit with wonder long before we entered here,
The symbol of the door ajar was pertinent and clear.
Upon the walls Salome danced as John walked from his cell,
And Jesus takes the apple as the First Man exits Hell.
The windows speak of harvesting the sower's planted seed,
And Crispin holds the severed head of every seeker's need.

A PAIR OF EYES

The Shepherd and the Lamb of God, the Chalice and the Light;
Both George and Michael glowing here in all their armoured might.
And yet the greatest beauty rested in another pane
And this depiction is the memory that will remain;
Of haunted eyes that plead with love for healing from the One,
Of faith that changed a Roman life and ministry begun.

A TEMPLE FLOOR

The windows glowed with stories, only one was all we saw,
Just like the Jester long ago, as on a chequered floor
An old man holds a Baby, while a sacrificial dove
Is One of Two his Mother holds beneath a Name above.
What story does this image tell, what secrets does it hold?
We feel that we have seen a glimpse of alchemical gold.

ABOUT THE AUTHORS

Sue Vincent is a Yorkshire born writer, poet and painter. Stuart France is a writer and essayist from Lancashire.

In spite of the historic division between the two counties, the writing partnership of France and Vincent has a peculiar alchemy of humour, scholarship and vision that has given birth to many books, including the *Triad of Albion, Doomsday* and *Lands of Exile* series'.

After decades of practical involvement with the magical and mystical traditions of the esoteric fraternity, France and Vincent are now directors of the Silent Eye, a School of Consciousness. As part of their commitment to the school, they run regular workshops in the landscape, details of which can be found on the Silent Eye website.

Together, they spend most of their free time exploring and cataloguing the ancient and sacred sites of Albion, seeking to understand their purpose and what they meant to those who built the ancient monuments and places of worship.

You can follow their adventures online at scvincent.com or franceandvincent.com and find Sue on Twitter @SCVincent.

If you have enjoyed this book, please consider leaving a review on Amazon or Goodreads.

THE SILENT EYE

The Silent Eye School of Consciousness is a modern Mystery School, founded by Steve Tanham, that celebrates the inherent magic in living and being.

With students around the world, the School offers a fully supervised and practical correspondence course that explores the self through guided inner journeys and daily exercises.

The Silent Eye also offers regular workshops that combine ritual, talks and informal gatherings within the landscape, bringing the teachings to life in a vivid and exciting format.

The Silent Eye operates on a not-for-profit basis.

Full details of the School, the distance learning course and upcoming events may be found on the official website: thesilenteye.co.uk.

OTHER BOOKS IN THIS SERIES
BY
STUART FRANCE AND SUE VINCENT

Triad of Albion

The Initiate   Heart of Albion   Giants Dance

Don and Wen thought it was just a day out in an ancient landscape wrought in earth and stone, walking the sacred ways of the Old Ones. They could not know what mysteries would unfold as the birds led them deep into the legendary history of Albion.

As the veils thin and waver, time shifts and the present is peopled with shadowy figures from the past, weaving their tales through a quest for understanding and opening wide the doors of perception for those who seek to see beyond the surface of reality...

Doomsday
The Ætheling Thing   Dark Sage   Scions of Albion

What exactly were the Norse gods doing on a supposedly Christian artefact that looked more like a standing stone than a cross?

Don is drawn to investigate, questioning the history of the Blessed Isles of Albion, while Wen determines to restore the position of one particular stone.

Which would have been alright if Ben hadn't gone back for the gun...

Lands of Exile
But 'n' Ben   Beck 'n' Call   Kith 'n' Kin

While Ben, fast becoming a folk hero, languishes in Bakewell Gaol, Don and Wen are on holiday... or 'on the run' if Bark Jaw-Dark and PC 963 Kraas, hot in pursuit, are to be believed.

From England to Scotland and Ireland, the officers of the Law follow the trail of the erratic couple.

But who is the shadowy figure, hovering beyond sight?

What is his interest in a small standing stone and just how many high-level strings can he pull... and why?

MORE BOOKS BY FRANCE AND VINCENT

Triad of Albion
The Initiate - Heart of Albion - Giants Dance

The Doomsday Series
The Ætheling Thing - Dark Sage - Scions of Albion

Lands of Exile
But 'n' Ben - Beck 'n' Call - Kith 'n' Kin

Graphic Novels
Mister Fox: The Legend
Mister Fox & the Demon Dogs
Mister Fox and the Green Man
Mister Fox: Winter's Tail

Loreweavers
An Imperious Impulse: Coyote Tales

Books by Stuart France

Poetry/mythology
Crucible of the Sun: The Mabinogion Retold

Spiritual Journey
The Living One: Caravan to Cairns

Philosophy
Slivers of Søren: Testaments to Truth
Pieces of Nietzsche: A Thinker's Bias
Nuances of Nicoll: The Keys to Heaven

Books by Sue Vincent

Mythology
The Osiriad: Myths of Ancient Egypt

Esoteric Fantasy
Swords of Destiny

Guided Meditations
Petals of the Rose

Poetry and humour
Notes from a Small Dog: Four Legs on Two
Laughter Lines: Life from the Tail End
Doggerel: Life with the Small Dog
Pass the Turkey!: Christmas with the Small Dog
Life Lines: Poems from a Reflection

With Dr G. Michael Vasey
The Mystical Hexagram: The Seven Inner Stars of Power

Available via Amazon worldwide